DOGGY STYLE

DOGGY STYLE

ALANA ALBERTSON

This book is dedicated to Jessica King, my partner in our dog rescue, Pugs N Roses. She's a boy mom, an amazing wife, and a great friend. She has selflessly saved hundreds of dogs. Love you, Jess.

The poor dog, in life the firmest friend. The first to welcome, foremost to defend.

LORD BYRON

DOGGY STYLE

When it comes to doggy style, he's behind you 100%.

Preston Evans is a legend in and out of the bedroom. He's six feet two, gorgeous, and famous because his celebrity ex Snapchatted him doing her doggy style. Even worse, to capitalize on his infamy, he opened a puppy store called Doggy Style. I don't care if his abs are chiseled, his arms are tattooed, and that his face belongs on the cover of a magazine. Every dog sold and bred means a shelter dog dead!

I chained myself to his store in protest, but instead of calling the cops, he threw me a bone.

If I help him open his puppy store, he'll transform it into a shelter dog adoption center, saving the lives of thousands of dogs. And then I will never have to see this sexy, dirty-talking jerk again. How hard can he—uh, I mean, it—be?

Sex is off the table. So why do I want him to bend me over it?

CHAPTER ONE

YESSI

I burst through the shelter's door at four fifty-five in the afternoon and almost retch from the smell of bleach and dog shit. You think I'd be used to it by now, but it always makes my eyes water. Damn Los Angeles traffic. I have five minutes. Five minutes left to save the lives of three of the dogs in the euthanasia room scheduled to be slaughtered.

The lobby is packed with irresponsible jerks waiting to surrender their pets. I blink back tears when I glance at an elderly Chihuahua with a wagging tail and a pink collar.

Dammit, this shelter is brimming with dogs. An old, tan Chihuahua doesn't stand a chance.

I know I risk getting arrested again if I interfere with the surrender, but I can't help myself.

I approach her owner. The man even looks like a douchecanoe, wearing a white wifebeater tank top and stained green cargo shorts. "Excuse me, sir. Do you realize that the second you sign over your dog, they're going to kill her? Before you leave the parking lot, she'll be taken away on a red leash, injected with poison, and then tossed in the bins in the back to be rendered into dog food."

The guy points his finger in my face. "I'm moving. I ain't got no choice."

His breath reeks of vodka and vomit. I resist the urge to recoil. "You've always got a choice. I'm begging you, mister. Please, she'll be murdered."

"You want her, lady?"

Don't look, Yessi. Don't look at the dog!

Like a rubbernecker fixating on a car crash, I look down and stare into the dog's sad eyes. She should be happily retired from her days of barking at the mailman, content to sit on a sofa and be loved. Instead, she's about to meet her end in a cold, dank cage, waiting for the kennel attendant to lead her to her death. Her sweet face will haunt me forever if I walk away.

No. I can't take another chi. They never get adopted. I'm over my dog limit. If animal control stops by my house one more time, I'll be evicted.

"I can't. I'm begging you to keep her. Don't you have a friend or family member who will take her?" I plead.

Loser shakes his head. "Nope."

He's next in line. That chi is a dead dog walking.

Don't do it, Yessi. You can't take another dog. You've already committed to pulling three dogs today.

I stand closer to the guy, toss back my hair, and stick out my tits. I'm not above flirting with him to save this dog's life. Forcing myself to touch his shoulder, I employ a sexy, breathy voice.

"Listen, I can tell you're a good man." I touch his tiny bicep for added effect. "But she'll die. I'm not lying. They will kill her. Today. If you give me a week, I may be able to find another foster. Please, please, give her a chance. If you ever loved this dog, please don't do this."

The guy stares right in between my tits. "Fine, lady. I'll give you twenty-four hours. But only because you're hot." He scribbles his number on a paper on the counter. "If you don't call me by tomorrow, I'm coming back here to leave her in the night drop."

Asshole. I grab his number. "Thank you. I'll find her a spot by tomorrow. What's her name? Is she good with other dogs, cats, and kids?"

He nods his head. "Yup. Her name is Gidget. Had her since she was a puppy. She's potty-trained and loves to cuddle. She wouldn't hurt a fly."

Then why are you dumping her, you piece of shit? I kneel down to snap a picture of Gidget and upload it to my rescue's Instagram page.

This is Gidget. Being surrendered today. Has twenty-four hours to find a foster or will DIE! #pugsnroses #rescuedog #adoptdontshop #chisofinstagram #chihuahuasofinstagram

I write down my number on another piece of paper and hand it to the guy. "Okay, I'm Yessi. Please call me before you dump her."

The guy eye-fucks me and then strides out of the shelter.

Gidget lives another day.

But only one day. I need to find her a place, stat.

Deb, the shelter director, sees me. She picks up her phone and makes a call to the back kennel. Once she hangs up, she barks at me, "They'll be right out. That'll be eighty dollars each."

Two hundred forty dollars to save three dogs? It was only supposed to be one hundred and sixty. My heart races as I quickly check the rescue's bank balance on my phone. One hundred and seventy-one dollars and thirty-two cents. Dammit. Last month we were wiped out by the medical bills from a sheltie who needed ACL surgery. We have donations coming in today, and we had a few adoptions last week, but the funds must not have gone through yet. I can't use my personal credit card again. It won't even go through—it's maxed.

But if I don't, one of these dogs will die.

I look back at Deb. "Did any of them come in fixed? Because then it would only be one hundred and sixty dollars."

She types something on the computer, and her eyes brighten. "Actually, yes. The beagle was spayed. One hundred and sixty it is."

I slap down the rescue's debit card.

Today's my lucky day. Actually, it's these three dogs' lucky day.

The kennel attendant comes out from the back room and hands me leashes attached to the three sorriest dogs I've ever seen—a one-eyed, black pug mix, followed by a senior beagle with a foul-smelling ear, and a limping miniature pinscher.

Three dogs I'll never adopt out. Three dogs destined to live in an overcrowded foster home while people waste their money purchasing purebred puppies. Three dogs who gave their best years to their owners, only to be dumped when they were no longer cute and fluffy.

But they don't know that. And I've just saved their lives.

I secure them with the leashes and harnesses I brought before I dash out of the shelter. The cries from the dogs in the back room who will be murdered today will ring in my head at night. And forever.

But I have to focus on the ones I can save.

Once inside my beat-up car that barely runs, I free the dogs from their crates and indulge in doggy kisses. The min pin cowers on the floor, the pug mix pukes all over my seat, and the beagle pees on my foot. Basically, my typical Saturday night.

I grab some old rags and clean up their messes. Now, it's off to the drive-thru for puppuccinos.

Is it too early for me to start drinking?

The dogs indulge in their treats, and the pug mix licks my face. That's the closest I'll get to some action anytime soon. Unlike Avril—one of my partners in this rescue—I never hook up. I can't even remember the last time I got laid. I'm not sure of the real reason for my lackluster sex life. Maybe it's because I hate online dating and would rather spend my nights on the sofa cuddling with my foster dogs than in a crowded bar meeting someone who's more interested in his phone than getting to know me. Avril even bought me a pillowcase that reads, *Sleeps with dogs*. Pathetic, but true.

As I'm pulling out of the parking lot, I call Avril. "Hey girl, got them. And we need to find an immediate foster for a chi."

She sighs. "Dammit, Yessi. I saw your Instagram post. We don't have an open foster. Eden's going to kill you. I have thirteen dogs at my house. Thirteen! I'd have better luck finding a unicorn."

She's right. Eden, the founder of the rescue, will flip. She's always lecturing Avril and me about responsible rescuing. What the hell is that? Sounds like an oxymoron. "Well, at least we could find a foster for a unicorn. Don't worry. That one is on me. She was just so cute. We shared a moment. I'll figure it out." My gut wrenches. No matter how many dogs I save, there's always another one about to be murdered.

Despite my best efforts, it's never enough.

I will never be enough.

Sometimes I wonder if my efforts matter at all because I can't even find a foster for a dog about to die. Or someone to watch my dogs when I need a break. Sure, Avril and Eden will. But they're in the same boat as me.

Sometimes, I wish I didn't care so much.

I take a deep breath. "Anyways, I'm dropping off the newbies at the vet, then heading home."

"Well, thanks for picking up the three. Are they adoptable?"

I look at the min pin shaking on my seat. I reach down to

pet him, and he bites me. I blot the blood with a straw wrapper. "Nope."

"Dammit. Get some cute pictures, and I'll network." She pauses and lowers her voice. "By the way, do you know who Preston Evans is?"

Preston Evans. Of course, I know all about Preston Evans. He's a legend. Not only is he ridiculously hot—sporting a fitness-model physique, dark wavy hair that begs women to run their fingers through it, and bedroom eyes that could seduce a nun—but he's also a war hero turned social media superstar. The guy has like half a million followers on Instagram. Ever since his celebrity ex Snapchatted a video of him doing her doggy style, Preston Evans has been everywhere. He even came out with a line of t-shirts reading, *I'm an animal, let's do it doggy style.* Hell, I own one of them. I can't even fathom how many women that man has bedded.

And unfortunately, I'm not one of them.

"Of course I know who he is. Why? Did you sleep with him?" She probably did. I would be so jealous.

"No. I wish. Did you hear that he's about to open a new puppy store on Main?"

What the hell? "Noooooooooo. What store?"

"It's called Doggy Style."

"Of course it is," I say, somberly. Normally I would laugh at the name choice, but my brain immediately realizes what a new puppy store will mean for all the local shelter dogs.

Fewer adoptions, and more dead dogs.

"Grand opening is next week. A bunch of us are going down there to protest when it opens. We're going to bring red paint and pour it over our heads to represent the blood of the shelter dogs who'll die because of the morons buying his puppies. Should be fun. Want to come?"

"Sounds like a blast. I'll be there. I hate people, Avril. I really do. You should've seen the guy with the chi. Didn't care at all that his dog was going to die. What's wrong with everyone?"

Most days, I fantasize about moving somewhere off the grid with my dogs, so I don't have to deal with the public. I can't handle the heartbreaking stories in the news every day. It just seems like no one cares anymore about anyone other than themselves.

"I agree. The world's insane, and it's getting worse. It'll be even harder for us to have successful adoption events with his store there. Maybe we should burn it down tonight, so it doesn't open."

I love how Avril just brings up arson like it's a logical solution. "You're nuts. Talk to you later."

"Bye, babe."

I turn down Katella Avenue and head to the vet clinic, which is where I spend most of my free time. We are so lucky to have them—they work on credit, allow us to board our dogs there for eight dollars a day until they're healthy enough to go to foster homes, and give us medical care at a huge discount.

The tech, Stace, greets me with a smile. She knows the routine. Shelter exam, fecal, dental, microchip, and all shots. When they're healthy enough, I'll pick them up and take them to their foster homes where they'll stay until they get adopted. I pray the dogs don't have a bad case of kennel cough.

Stace shines a light into the black pug mix's remaining eye. "Well, at least his other eye looks good. I'll have the doctor examine him. What's his name?"

I think for a second and partake in a few more pug kisses. "Pirate. Let's call the beagle Lucy, and the min pin Nemo."

"Sounds like a plan. I'll text you when I have an update."

I say goodbye and leave the vet. Time to head to the liquor store to buy some booze so I can drink myself into oblivion.

How is this my life? Three years ago, I offered to help pull a dog from a shelter for a rescue that had posted a plea on Facebook. Now I help run a dog rescue and spend all my free time transporting dogs, conducting home checks, answering emails, and dealing with flaky fosters. My personal life has been in shambles ever since my boyfriend left me last year because he said I cared more about the dogs than I did about him. I'm broke from all the veterinary bills from my own dogs that I've adopted—or, well, inherited after they didn't get adopted. My day job as a tattoo artist, while creatively fulfilling, doesn't even cover my living expenses in pricey Orange County.

At least it's summer. But then again, it's always summer in the OC. And summer means the Fourth of July—D-day for dog rescuers. So many dogs get lost after the fireworks and even more are killed because the shelters fill up. I used to love the Fourth—and now it's my least favorite holiday.

I really need a vacation.

Not that I plan on going on one. I haven't had a break in years. I'm dying to attend the pet expo conference in Hawai'i this weekend. There's going to be all these great seminars on rescue strategies, finding grants, and fundraising. But I can't afford the ticket, and it's impossible to find a pet sitter because I have eleven dogs at my house—six of my own and five fosters.

I drive down Main Street in search of the closest liquor store, but then the glare of a neon-pink sign stops me.

Doggy Style.

Preston's puppy store.

Who opens a puppy store in this day and age? Millions of dogs are murdered daily in shelters. Sweet, amazing dogs, including purebred dogs and puppies. There's never, ever an excuse to breed or buy when shelter pets die every day.

I pull over and find parking. Once I walk over to the shop, I peer into the window.

Puppies.

Puppies everywhere.

Pug puppies panting, goldendoodles gallivanting, British bulldogs barking. Next week, the residents of Huntington Beach will be snatching up these puppies. Meanwhile, I can't find a single foster family and have twenty dogs in the rescue who desperately need forever homes.

I see someone walk toward the back of the store. A tall, dark, handsome figure who I recognize immediately.

My chest constricts—Preston Evans is inside.

I should smash in the window. That would get his attention.

But that would also get me thrown in jail.

Hmm. I ponder my options for a bit, then it hits me.

I return to my car, open the passenger door, and pop open my glove box, retrieving a pair of pink, fuzzy handcuffs. My ex and I had been into some light bondage. I'd finally collected my stuff from him the other week and had been too lazy to clean out my car.

And now these restraints will serve a higher purpose.

I grab the cuffs, a bottle of water, plus my purse and walk back to the store.

I take a deep breath and clamp the cold metal against my wrist, the familiar tightness causing my heart to race. I take the other end of the cuffs and place it on the door handle. The clink of metal against the steel exhilarates me as the handcuffs give one click of finality.

Preston Evans will not open his store.

He'll have to get through me first.

And I'm not going to go down without a dogfight.

CHAPTER TWO

PRESTON

"Preston!" Hugh, my business partner, yells at me from the showroom. "Get your ass out here. There's some deranged chick handcuffed to the front of our store. She probably wants you to bone her."

What the fuck? My stomach knots and I pray Kira didn't hear Hugh's shouting through the phone. "But you promised you'd go to the pet expo with me and then help me with the grand opening. You are so good with dogs," I plead to her.

"Whatever, Preston. I agreed to help you *before* we broke up. It would be awkward now. I can't go to Hawai'i with my ex."

My chest tightens. I need this store to be successful. "I'm not trying to get back together with you. We weren't right for each other. But you could still help out me—as a friend."

She makes a noise that I can't decipher as a laugh or a huff. "We will always be friends, but I don't think us going to a romantic island and working together is a great idea right now."

But I need you. "You promised to help me. You can't just flake on me two days before we are supposed to go."

"Yeah, sorry about that. I've been asked to do a charity yoga event. I'm sure you can find someone else to go with you and also help you open your store. Maybe you can ask the girl handcuffed outside your store."

Great. She definitely heard.

"Really funny. Take care, Kira."

"Bye, Pres."

Dammit. I'm screwed. I don't know anything about dogs. Hell, I don't even own one, though I was close to Kira's beagle, Lady. I loved that damn dog, but I haven't seen Lady, or Kira since we broke up a few months ago.

I knock back the rest of my beer, toss the bottle in the trash, and contemplate my options. I scroll through my Instagram like it's LinkedIn and pray that I can find someone I know who loves dogs. Maybe a pet groomer or a sexy veterinarian or a kickass dog trainer.

But it can't just be anyone. I need a dog whisperer with a ton of followers, so I can get the word out about my business and impress investors and vendors at the expo. Someone who is interesting, smart, and cool, since I have to travel and work with her. I don't want to be stuck with some vapid, materialistic woman. I could hire a man, I suppose, but I already am working with Hugh so it would be nice to have some feminine energy around the shop.

Should I post an ad? Contact some friends? I'm a leader, decisive in every aspect of my life. For once, I have no idea what to do about this mess.

But for now, I have to take care of the situation outside.

Damn these groupies.

Don't get me wrong—I appreciate their attention, and I'm grateful for their support but being a social media super-star is as much of a blessing as it is a curse. The worst part of the overexposure is that I can no longer figure out if a woman likes me for me or if she is just using me to grow her own following.

I miss the art of seduction. That initial spark when I first see a woman I want. Flirty banter while I'm pursuing her. Planning a romantic first date. The anticipation before the first kiss and, then, ultimately, seducing her. I love the chase. Everything is too easy these days. With a swipe right, I can get laid in twenty minutes, without even having to work for it.

I emerge from the back room and walk into the main showroom of our new store, Doggy Style. If someone had told me three years ago when I was still a grunt in the Marine Corps that I would someday become the star of a sex video and be a guy who pimps puppies, I never would've believed it. But, one could say, my life has gone to the dogs. The video that Kira broadcast of me fucking her went viral. At first, I had been furious with her. Not that I was embarrassed. Fuck no. I'm a beast in the bedroom.

Or on the floor.

Or, like in the video, over a table.

But I knew the footage would make it a struggle to find

certain sponsorships. Sure, the entertainment industry embraced me, but the serious business investors have turned their back on me.

Even so, that video has changed my life. And I'm rolling with it. My line of Doggy Style t-shirts and merchandise have blown up. I'm making a killing. Opening this store is the next part of my world domination.

I pause and take in the space. I must admit that the place looks awesome. Doggy couture hangs on the racks, sparkly collars are displayed in cases, and pet art decorates the walls.

But the highlight of Doggy Style is our puppies.

Two dozen purebred puppies are artistically placed in designer plastic crates against the wall but, unlike some puppy stores, we are treating every dog wonderfully. Our puppies receive the best food, toys, and medical care that money can buy.

Hugh, who is also my childhood best friend, stands at the front of the store, peering out the window. Dude is nothing like me. I'm tall; he's short. I spend hours in the gym; he spends hours playing Xbox. I love to surf; the guy can't swim. But he's my right-hand man. This entire store concept was his idea, and I am happy to run it with him, but he doesn't know anything about dogs either. We just figured that this would be a good business opportunity to capitalize on my notoriety.

I slap Hugh on the back. "Where is she?"

"There. She keeps chanting 'Save the dogs!' I think she's one of those psycho animal protestors."

Great. Just what I need. Bad publicity. But I've learned the hard way that any buzz is a good buzz.

When I squint through the frosted glass window, my feelings of disgust melt into desire.

Handcuffed to our front door is a stunningly beautiful woman. She has waist length black hair that touches her incredibly round ass, her full breasts fill out her tight black T-shirt, her plump pink lips are begging to be kissed, and her long eyelashes slay me. Her left arm has a kickass *Catrina* tattoo—a sexy skeleton girl with a cross on her forehead and a red rose under her chin.

I unlock the door, step outside, and give her a smile. "If you wanted to meet me, you could've just knocked."

At the sound of my voice, she jumps to her feet. The

moment her dark eyes meet mine, I see her breath falter slightly. Her pupils flare with hunger.

This sniper has found his prey.

Our moment exists for mere seconds, and her look of lust is replaced by rage. A scowl crosses her face, and she lashes back at me. "Meet you? Wow, you are so arrogant. Why on earth would I want to meet a womanizing fame whore who sells puppies? You are disgusting."

A womanizing fame whore? I'm not a cheater: I had been faithful and loyal to Kira. And, now, I'm single. But damn. Hugh's right. She is one of those animal activists. Maybe she's posed naked for a PETA ad? Note to myself: get her name and Google her.

I point to the cuffs. "Got a key for those? Or should I saw them off? Hey, if you are into some BDSM, I'm your man."

She spits at me.

I wipe my face. Man, she's a feisty one.

"You'll never be my man. And I'm not leaving until you stop selling puppies here. Do you know that 1.5 million animals are killed in shelters every year?"

I've heard that number thrown around before, but I'm

pretty sure it's exaggerated. Kira had been involved in rescuing beagles from laboratories, but I don't know too much about shelter dogs. "Look, people will always buy puppies. Our dogs come from good breeders. Would you like to see the dogs?"

She laughs at me. A few people walking down the street stop to stare at her as her voice gets louder.

"Oh, I know all about your dogs. I spend my life rescuing their mothers who are crammed in steel crates until they are drowned at puppy auctions when they can no longer breed. And there's no such thing as a responsible breeder. It's an oxymoron. Actually, you're the fucking moron. You don't have any clue what you are talking about!"

Whoa. Her face is red, and she bares her teeth at me like a rabid dog. But underneath her fury, I see determination. Dedication to her cause. A look that I recognize from the battlefield.

I have many faults, but overreacting isn't one of them. As a sniper, I have been trained to remain calm under pressure. And this beautiful woman is clearly enraged. I refuse to antagonize her further.

"Hey, relax. What's your name?"

"Don't you tell me to relax. Saving dogs is my life. I run a rescue. I saved three dogs today from a shelter a few miles from here on their last day of life. Hundreds of dogs die there daily. And there is nothing I can do. And now because of your stupid store, even more will be slaughtered."

Her voice is choked with emotion. And for the first time since Hugh came up with the idea to open the store, I question whether I'm doing the right thing.

But, of course, I am. I swallow my doubt. We did our research. Found the best breeders. This is America. Everyone should have a choice about where to purchase his or her pet from. I risked my life in Iraq for our freedom.

"Let's start over. I'm Preston Evans. Tell you what, if you uncuff yourself, I'll listen to everything you have to say. Let me take you to dinner. There's a great little restaurant down the street."

Her beautiful eyes open wide. "Dinner? With you? No. That's out of the question. I'm not going anywhere with you. I won't let you open this store."

I touch her shoulder, and she flinches. I raise my hands in mock surrender. "I get that, but I'm a businessman. I'm willing to listen to your points and facts, and then I'll make an educated decision. I'm not promising anything. That's the best I can do. Take it or leave it."

She shakes her head. "No. I see the puppies inside. You won't change your mind. I know about you—I've seen your Instagram. All you care about is how many followers you have, and you are not above exploitative tactics to get them. Now hundreds of dogs are going to die as a direct result of your disgusting store."

I take a step back and study her. Ever since that video was released, no one—and I mean no one—other than my father has stood up to me. Not Hugh. Not even Kira. I'm surrounded by "yes" men and "Oh, yes!" women. It's refreshing to meet someone who isn't impressed by me at all. Someone who despises me.

A challenge.

"What's your name, sweetheart?"

She tugs on the handcuffs. "Don't call me sweetheart. That's degrading."

"How is *sweetheart* degrading? I didn't call you *bitch*. Would it offend you, too, if I held your door open for you?"

"It's uncomfortably intimate. I don't know you, nor do I want to."

Man, she's a piece of work. "Fine. What's your name, and what is the name of your dog rescue?"

She bites her lip. "My name is Yesenia Cordova. I'm a tattoo artist, but I'm also the adoption coordinator for Pugs N Roses. We are a 501(c)(3) nonprofit dog rescue here in Huntington Beach."

As she speaks, I can't resist eye fucking her. Not only is she gorgeous, but she is unlike any woman I've met lately. She has a style of her own: badass Latina. I take in every inch of her. From her mile-long eyelashes hanging over her whiskey-brown eyes to her tight jeans and plain black t-shirt covered in dog hair. I feel a twinge of jealousy over the dogs who must've been nestled on her chest. I shake myself out of it.

"Nice to meet you, Yesenia. Why don't you tell me what you want?"

"What I want is for you to stop selling puppies at your store. Once you agree, I'll leave you alone. If you don't agree, I'll be your worst nightmare. I'll be down here every week with a slew of protestors making your life a living hell."

Ha. I almost laugh in her face but keep it to myself. "I can just have you arrested."

"The cops aren't going to arrest peaceful protestors. I'm serious. There is a secret rescue network, and we are all crazy. Batshit, actually. We will ruin your business. We've shut down shops before, and I can't wait to shut down yours, too."

Ah fuck. Protestors hadn't crossed my mind when I agreed to open the store, and we already have agreements and contracts with breeders across the country.

"What's in it for me?"

Her face contorts. "What do you mean? You want a reward for being a decent human being and not contributing to the slaughter of homeless pets?"

"If I stop selling purebred puppies in here, what will you do for me?"

She shakes her head. "You are even worse than I thought you'd be. Sorry, Preston, I'm not going to suck your cock."

The way she says cock sends a jolt to mine. I love her filthy mouth. She is delicious.

I have to fuck her.

But as beautiful as she is, her beauty is marred by sadness. Instead of looking hopeful and bright, her eyes hide pain.

I grab my phone and search for her profile on Instagram. A Yessi Cordova pops up instantly, and I notice that she follows me. A quick perusal of her feed and I'm impressed. Beautiful artwork, quotes, pictures with dogs, and, most importantly, thirteen thousand followers. I click on a post and notice it received six hundred and forty-six likes.

I show her my phone opened to her profile. "Nice feed."

"Well, enjoy it for now. I'll be blocking your profile."

Ha.

Then an idea springs into my mind.

Maybe I can alleviate her pain, and she can help me with my business. She would be perfect. She spends all her time with dogs, and she can get the other rescuers off my back. Working with a dog rescuer who has a big following will do wonders for my PR.

And I'd love to see her in a bikini in Hawai'i.

But it won't be easy to get her to agree to help me. I mean why should she? She clearly is appalled by my existence.

There has to be some Achilles heel that will get her to help me out.

I check Instagram again, this time heading to her rescue page. I see a picture of a sorry looking chihuahua with a pink collar.

Bingo.

I follow her and her rescue on Instagram, and then I put my phone in my pocket. "I changed my mind about dinner."

She exhales loudly. I think I see a flash of disappointment but a second later it is gone. "Good. I didn't want to go anyway."

"What are you going to do about that dog you posted on your rescue page?"

Her lips tremble. "I don't know. You should've seen her owner. He was wasted. He didn't care at all that she was going to die. I don't have anywhere to take her."

This is almost too easy.

I smile. "I'll take her."

"What?"

"I said, I'll take her. She can stay at the store. I'll get her ready for the grand opening."

"Are you ser . . . serious? Do you have any dogs of your own?"

"Yes, I'm serious. And no, I don't have any dogs of my own. Not yet. I want to help this dog out. Where is she?"

"She's still with her owner. Actually, I'm freaking out about it. I'm afraid he's going to dump her at the shelter night drop tonight."

The night drop? For animals? Is there such a thing? Dogs, discarded like trash? Maybe she's exaggerating. I push the thought of dogs and cats, abandoned, locked in cages, in some cold, abandoned building out of my head.

I place my hand on Yessi's back. "Let's go get her."

"You want to come with me to pick her up? That's not necessary. If you are serious about fostering her, I can go get her now and bring her to you, but I don't need you to go with me."

Unbelievable—she doesn't even want me to go with her to pick up a dog I will be fostering. "You just told me that the guy was wasted and might dump her in the night drop. You are gorgeous, and you are going to drive out somewhere to meet him to get the dog? He could rape you. Do you normally drive out at night to meet strange men and rescue dogs?"

She nods her head. "Yup."

I shake mine. "Well, if I'm fostering this dog, I'm going with you to get her."

"I don't want to spend time with you. You are just as much of a stranger to me as her owner is. For all I know, you could be a serial killer."

Well, that's a first. I lower my voice and stare into her eyes. "You know I'm not a serial killer. I'm a highly decorated former Marine. You even said you know about me, and I can see you follow me on Instagram. And believe it or not, I am a gentleman. I'm not going to take advantage of you."

"You really want to foster her? I would prefer for her to stay at your place instead of the store, but because I'm desperate, your store will do if that's my only option. But only temporarily until I find a full-time at-home foster. It's better for the dog to be placed in a home setting so the foster can get the dog ready for adoption."

"I'm fine with all that. She can stay at my place."

She exhales, and her shoulders relax. "You will need to fill out a foster application, and I'm going to have to do a home check to make sure she's safe. I need to see if you have a secure fence and if you have a pool that there is a gate."

I smirk. "I guess that answers the question, 'Your place or mine.'"

She rolls her eyes. "I'm not amused."

"I'm kidding. Lighten up. I'll give you the tour of my crib after we get her, and I'm happy to fill out an application. Let's go get her now before that jerk dumps her."

She throws her hands up in defeat. "Fine. We can go get her, you can foster her. But I'm still going to protest your fucking puppy store. We are not cool. Got it, buddy?"

I love her bossy streak. I can't wait to tame her—pull her hair, slap her ass, and make her submit to me.

I tug on her cuffs. "Yes, ma'am. Now, where are the keys?"

She reaches into her pocket and tosses them to me. I quickly release her, and she puts her hands out to collect the cuffs, but I stick them in my back pocket. "I'll keep these, for later."

"In your dreams, Evans. I'll call the guy and find a place for us to meet the dog."

"I'm going to run inside and grab my keys. I'll be back out in five minutes."

"Lucky me." She grabs her phone and dials as I go inside.

Hugh stops me when I step back inside. "What was that all about?"

I laugh. "You were right. Some crazy protestor. But I handled her."

"Good job, bro. Next time just call the cops."

I shake my head. "Not necessary. I'm fostering a dog for her. And I want her to go to the expo with me and help us with the store. Kira backed out, and this woman hasn't agreed yet. Hell, I haven't even asked her, but she will."

"What? Fuck Kira, man. She promised us. And you want some crazy chick to work in our shop? And go to Hawai'i with you? Well, those crazy bitches are great in bed."

"You're an asshole, dude. But she'd be perfect. She has a ton of followers on Instagram and runs a dog rescue, so she must know a lot about dogs. And if she vouches for us, hopefully, the activists will leave our shop alone. I dig her."

"Whatever, dude. I don't know who is crazier—you or her."

"Probably me," I say as I head back to my office.

I grab my keys and walk outside. Yessi is standing there, her hair glowing in the moonlight. She actually gives me a smile.

She touches my arm. "Hey, thanks for fostering her. You saved her life."

CHAPTER THREE

YESSI

My hand shakes as I reach for my keys. What on earth had just happened?

One minute, I was handcuffed to the door of Preston's puppy store, and next thing I know, he has offered to foster a dog for me. Now we are on our way to pick the dog up. Why was he offering to help me? This is a guy who is about to sell puppies for a living, and now he's going to foster an old chihuahua? He has to have an ulterior motive. If he thinks I'll stop harassing his pet store, he's dead wrong. I'm not going to back off. I'll still be there protesting every day.

And that way, I can still look at him. What? Don't judge me. I'm a hot-blooded American woman.

Dammit—why does he have to be so ridiculously hot? I mean everything about him is perfection. His tousled dark hair is shiny, his skin is tanned, his arms are ripped and covered by tattoos. Decent tattoos, too. Hell, I'd love to ink him up myself. Maybe I'll tattoo my name on his ass.

Stop lusting after him, Yessi. He's the enemy!

I take a calming breath and think about all the dogs who will die as a direct result of his pet store. Rage pulses through my veins.

Okay. Back to hating him.

Preston places his hand on my wrist; his touch immediately causes my heart to beat faster. "Let's take my truck."

"No. We can go in my car."

He doesn't argue, and I walk in front of him. But when we reach my car, I look in and see the dried vomit stains and dog hair covered seats.

"On second thought, we can go in your car."

He smiles, and I notice his dimples. Drown your heart in the ocean dimples which highlight a movie star smile. It's unreal.

"Sounds like a plan. I'm parked up the block."

He leads me toward a side street. A group of ladies is walking toward us on the sidewalk, and they all simultaneously giggle when they see him, not that I can blame them. Like I said, dude is hot.

But Preston doesn't even seem to check them out. Instead, he places his hand on the swell of my back, and I resist the urge to push it off of me. In fact, it's quite the opposite—I enjoy his touch, despite myself.

One of the girls squints at him as she gets closer to us. "Oh my god! You're Preston Evans! Hi. I'm Gigi. Can I take a selfie with you?"

"Nice to meet you, Gigi. Sure, you can."

I step away from him, so his fans can fawn over him, but he pulls me to his side, and I end up in the damn picture with him.

Great. My reputation is ruined. I pray I don't get tagged in that photo, not that anyone would recognize me. If a rescuer sees that picture, I'll be ostracized from the community.

"Ladies, I'm holding a grand opening for my pet store,

Doggy Style, next week. I would love for you all to join us."

I quickly separate from him. "Us? I won't be there. I'll be outside protesting." I speak directly to the women. "If you all want a dog, I run a rescue, Pugs N Roses. We have plenty of amazing dogs who need homes."

The girls completely ignore me. Maybe I'm invisible.

"We'll be there for sure. Nice to meet you, Preston."

"Good night, ladies." Preston walks away from the group, and I reluctantly follow him.

You are doing this for Gidget. You don't have to like him.

"Does that ever annoy you?"

He shakes his head. "No. Not when they are sweet. Sometimes, if they are really drunk, I get annoyed. But I'm just grateful that having fans has given me the opportunity to support myself. After I got out of the Corps, I was a little lost."

Wow. I'm surprised at how open he is with his answer. I wonder how he met Kira. She had already been a reality star. But I don't want to ask too many questions about him. I just want to give him the dog and move on with my life. And I still plan to work on a more permanent foster for Gidget. I don't want to be tied to Preston. Being in his presence rattles me.

He walks up to a brand new shiny black Ford truck and opens the door for me. I literally bite my tongue to stop myself from chastising him for opening my door. This is not a date. This is a dog rescue mission. Or Paw Patrol as Avril's niece always says.

But then I think back to what Preston said earlier about me being offended because he called me sweetheart. What is wrong with me? Why am I so bitchy? Yes, he is selling dogs, and I have a reason to dislike him, but these days I seem to fight with everyone.

I force myself to say thanks.

"Where to?"

I resist the urge to cop a feel of his bicep and instead type the address into his navigation system.

He reads the screen and gives me a side eye. "You were honestly going to go there by yourself tonight? That's a super seedy area. How do you know he is even going to give you the dog? Maybe he's going to lure you there and rape you?"

Well, isn't Preston a ray of sunshine. "Why are you so

paranoid, dude? The guy just wants to dump his dog. He's not going to hurt me. Besides, I have mace in my purse."

He laughs. "Mace? By the time you grab it, he could attack you. Too bad I don't have my gun."

"Gun? Oh, of course, you have a gun."

"I'm a Marine. A sniper. Of course, I have a gun."

This guy can't possibly be more wrong for me. There is no way we have anything in common. Then why is his strong earthy scent intoxicating me?

I roll down the window and look outside. I'm not in the mood for small talk, so I just focus on the traffic.

"How did you get into dog rescue?"

"Nope. We aren't going to do this. I'm not going to just open up and create an emotional bond with you. I appreciate you for being willing to temporarily foster this dog, and I vow to get her into a permanent foster home as soon as possible, so I don't have to see you. But then again, fostering a homeless dog is the least you could do for opening a pet store."

"Gotcha."

That shuts him up pretty fast. He enters the freeway, and

we spend the rest of the ride in silence. After almost thirty minutes, he exits inland. Damn, he is right—this isn't the best area. I don't admit it to him, but I'm grateful that he is with me.

I text the owner that we are outside his apartment complex.

Preston jumps out of his truck. I attempt to open my own door, but he does it before I can. I'm still shocked by his gentlemanly behavior. I have not been pleasant to him. I'm not sure why he continues to be so nice to me.

The guy with the dog stands out front, holding little Gidget on a leash. She wags her tail. Poor girl, she probably thinks she's going on a walk. Little does she know she's about to be ripped from the only home she has ever known. And that her owner almost led her to her death.

I don't feel the need to greet this guy. "Do you have any paperwork for her? Shot records? Favorite toys? Her bed?"

"Nope."

Figures.

Preston kneels down and pets the dog. She immediately licks his hand. I try not to react, but my stone-cold heart melts a little bit.

I have the owner fill out the relinquishment form on our website from my phone.

Preston looks up at him. "Why are you giving her up?"

"I'm moving." The owner stares at Preston. "Hey, aren't you the dude who fucked that hot chick? You're the man. Are you fucking this bitch too? She's fucking fine."

I want to deck the guy. I even go as far as clenching my fist, but Preston holds me back.

"Yeah, that was me. But she wasn't just some hot chick. She was my girlfriend, and I loved her. And not that it's any of your business, but no I am not fucking this beautiful woman. I'm going to foster your dog, so she isn't murdered doesn't at the shelter. Apologize to Yessi now for calling her a bitch, or I'll beat the living shit out of you."

Oh my god! Swoon!

"Sorry, lady. I didn't mean anything by it."

I don't accept his apology.

"We're done here." Preston scoops Gidget up in his arms, puts his arm around my shoulders and leads me to the truck, where he once again opens the door.

Once back inside the truck, Gidget cuddles in my lap and gives me kisses.

I need to get away from Preston as soon as possible. I'm clearly not thinking straight, and the last thing I need is to go to his house to do a home check. "Thanks for going with me. I can actually text the vet tech and see if she can open up the clinic and take her tonight, so she can be vetted first thing in the morning. Then I can pick her up tomorrow, and we can do the home check then. Actually, Avril, the foster coordinator usually does the home checks. I can have her arrange to deliver you Gidget when she is ready." Granted Avril will probably fuck him, but unlike me, she won't get attached. Avril doesn't do relationships.

"That won't work. I head to Hawai'i in two days, so I want the dog acclimated to my place as soon as possible. Plus, there is no reason for her to spend the night in the clinic. But don't worry, my buddy Hugh is staying at my place when I'm gone. Gidget will be fine there. And we have a vet coming into the shop tomorrow, so I'll bring her to work to get her checked out. I'll pay for everything."

Hawai'i? Was he going to the pet expo? I didn't want to ask.

Well, doesn't he have it all figured out. I'm super jealous

that he is going to the pet expo, but I'm not about to tell him that.

"Okay. Well, let's go back to your store, and I'll get my car and then follow you back to your place."

"There's limited parking at my place because it's near the beach."

Of course, it's on the beach.

"Fine. Can we grab some food on the way over? I'm starving." And I am. I have barely eaten all day.

"Well, I'd love for you to join me for dinner. There is this little Thai restaurant a block away from my place. Maybe we could get takeout since we should get this dog home."

Fine. I give up. "Thai's fine. But I'm vegan, so I'll order."

"Great."

He gives me the name of the place, and I peruse the menu. I order a few items, he tells me what to add for himself, and twenty minutes later, he runs inside the restaurant to get the food while I stay in the truck with Gidget. I pet her and rub her belly. Tears well in my eyes when I realized that she would've been killed tonight if I hadn't intervened.

And if Preston hadn't offered to foster her.

A few minutes later, he emerges from the place with a few bags. Then we take off in his truck, and he enters a parking garage for his place.

Right on the beach.

This is going to be some home check.

CHAPTER FOUR

PRESTON

I park my truck, grab the bags of food, and exit the truck. Yessi has already opened her own door and is walking Gidget.

I lead them to an outdoor patch of grass and Gidget squats and pees.

Yessi pets her. "Good girl, Gidget. Her owner said she was potty trained, but it will take her a while to understand your routine. I'd take her out a couple of times tonight and first thing in the morning."

"Sounds like a plan. Come on. I'll show you my place."

We enter the elevator, and once the door opens to my floor, Yessi's mouth drops when she sees the view of the ocean.

"You actually live here? You clearly don't need the money. Why are you opening a puppy store?"

"It's an investment." She rolls her eyes. Time to change subjects. "I'll give you the tour."

I show her the kitchen, the balcony which is enclosed by glass, and my favorite room, my bedroom.

"Well, Gidget hit the lottery. Too bad you won't keep her. You should consider adopting her. She won't take up much room. Why don't you have any yourself?"

Good question. I definitely needed to own a dog. It would be good for my brand. "My ex had a beagle, and we were going to get another dog, but we broke up. I might pick one of the English Bulldog puppies in my store. English bulldogs are mascots for the Marines."

Her jaw gapes. "I can't believe you don't even have your own dog. So, you are just using them for profit like the Amish breeders do? You are the worst. Why the hell are you opening a dog store if you don't even have a dog yourself?"

"Because of my t-shirt line, Doggy Style. It's my brand."

Her brows snap together. "This is just some gimmick to you. These dogs are living, breathing animals, not just props for your 'brand.' Do you know where your beautiful bullies come from? Their moms spend their lives in cages and then they are sold at auction when they can no longer breed. Puppies born with any deformities are drowned."

I wince and try to push the images of dogs suffering out of my mind. Yessi was so passionate and convincing that I was beginning to doubt my business model. But I had found the best breeders. There is no way the moms of the dogs I purchased live like that.

Or do they?

Time to change the subject.

"So, am I approved?"

"Yes. I don't have a valid reason to deny you. But honestly, Gidget deserves better than you. At least your place is amazing." She looks at her watch. "I need to get going and feed my own dogs."

"Let's eat, first." I set the table, pop open a beer for myself, and offer her a glass of wine.

"No, thanks. I'll just have the Thai iced tea."

I wonder if she doesn't drink, or she just doesn't want to drink with me.

We sit at my little bistro table. I should hate this girl who clearly is disgusted by my very existence, but something about her fascinates me. Most of the girls I meet these days only care about themselves. Yessi has devoted her life to caring for the voiceless.

I follow her gaze to the ocean. Though she's clearly impressed by my place, she doesn't appear to be materialistic. I can tell that her jeans are not designer and she's not wearing any expensive jewelry.

After a few moments of uncomfortable silence, she finally speaks up.

"The food was great. Thank you."

"You're welcome."

She looks over at Gidget who is nestled on my sofa in a ball, snoring heavily, like she belongs there. "Why are you going to Hawai'i?"

"I'm going to the pet expo."

She purses her lips. "I'm jealous. I've always wanted to go. There is a big rescuer symposium. I bet I could learn about how to get grants and find more fosters."

Bingo. I push back my chair and take another swig of my beer.

"Then come with me."

Her eyelashes flip up, and I'm drawn into her beautiful eyes. "You're crazy."

"I'm serious. All expenses paid. You can go to your rescuer events, and I can network."

She shakes her head. "Nope. No way. Why would you even want me to go with you? In case you can't tell, I don't like you. Like at all."

I smirk. "I can tell. But you don't know me. I'm pretty sure if you gave me a chance, you'd see that I'm a good man. I'll make you a deal. I'll consider stopping the sale of pure-bred puppies at my store, and I'll take you to the Pet Expo if you help me open Doggy Style. We need someone who is good with dogs, and clearly, you know everything about them."

"Is this some joke to you? Your store is full of puppies. You are going to stop selling them if some random girl helps you open your store? Not to mention I would never, ever work in a store selling puppy mill dogs. That's like asking a nun to work in a strip club."

Ha. She's hilarious. I picture her in a habit which covers up some sexy lingerie.

She's clearly going to make this hard. But I know what I want.

I want Yessi to help run my store. And I want her to come to Hawai'i with me. It's a win-win. She clearly knows a lot about dogs, probably more than my ex does, and if Yessi works with me then she can keep these protesters off my back. The investors I have meetings with in Hawai'i will trust me more if they think I'm linked to a charity.

Yup, I have to make her agree. I'll sweeten the pot.

"I'll also make a tax-deductible donation to your rescue for twenty-five thousand dollars. Do we have a deal?"

Her eyes at first widen, but then she rolls them. "Are you serious? You can't just buy people. I can't take money from you. I'm not one of your Instagram disciples who will hop into your bed when you send them an emoji."

I dig this chick more and more. Every time she tells me no makes the hunt that much sweeter. "Look, it's up to you. I'm opening the store with the purebred puppies we already have. I can't return them to their breeders. But I could possibly be swayed to stop using breeders in the future and to feature shelter dogs instead. You could show me how."

She pulls at her hair and glances around as if she's

searching for answers. She's considering my offer. I need to throw in some more incentives, though twenty-five thousand dollars should be incentive enough. But this woman seems to be motivated by more than just money. I think for a second, and then I throw her a bone.

"How many dogs do you have in your rescue?"

"Twenty in the entire rescue. I have six fosters, Avril has seven, and Eden has four. Then there are three at the vet."

I quickly do the math in my head. Damn, that's a lot of dogs. "I'll make you a deal. You help me open this store, and I will let you host adoption events for all of your rescue dogs there. For the opening, you can bring all twenty, twenty-one including this chi, to the store, and we will showcase them. If you can convince me about the breeders, I'll strongly consider turning Doggy Style into a rescue only store. But if you say no, then I'll see you protesting daily. I'll even bring you coffee. Do you like it black or are you one of those women who likes pretty latte art?"

"Black, unless you have oat milk."

What the fuck is oat milk? Right, she's vegan.

She sizes me up, and I can see she is seriously contemplating saying yes.

"I'll find oat milk. Hell, I'll make it myself. Is that a yes?"

"No. I can't get the time off, and I can't afford to lose my job. I take no money from the rescue—all our donations go to the vet care of our dogs. I can't."

"Valid point. Do you like your tattoo shop?"

She shrugs. "It's okay. The owner is kind of a jerk, but it's fine. One day I want to open my own shop with vegan ink."

Vegan ink? I have plenty of tattoos and I never once heard of whether or not the ink used was vegan. "Well, my Marine Corps buddy has a shop a few blocks away. I'm not sure if his ink is vegan, but I'm sure you can bring your own. I can get you in there after my store opens. Or I can give you a job in my shop. I'll double your salary."

Her eyes focus on me and then she looks away. "This is crazy. You could find another manager. Someone who can stand being around you. Why do you want me to work here? You know nothing about me."

"I'll be honest. My ex was supposed to help me out and go with me to the pet expo, but she just flaked, literally minutes before I met you. And then I found you hand-cuffed to my store. Perfect timing, I'd say. I checked your Instagram profile outside the store, and you have a good following. We will be doing a bunch of social media promotion. You also run a dog rescue, so you probably are great with dogs, and then maybe your whack job activist friends won't sabotage my business."

She shifts on her feet. I probably shouldn't have insulted her activist friends, but it's too late to take my words back. I feel like I've made some progress, but I can't tell if she's going to agree one way or another.

"I don't have a pet sitter for my own dogs, and I won't be able to find a foster to take in the others. I just can't."

In the Marine Corps, I learned how to solve any obstacle that was placed in my way. She wants to take my offer—I just need to make it easy for her. "How many dogs do you have at your place?"

Her eyes narrow, and she bites her bottom lip.

"Tell me. I'm not animal control."

"Eleven," she whispers and looks down at her sandals. I study her toes—they are painted electric purple and have black rhinestones on them. My mouth waters. I know she has a freaky side that I can't wait to discover. "But six are my own dogs."

I must really be desperate for this gig because I can't

believe the next words that I'm about to say. "You can bring all eleven there—we have plenty of kennels. That way we can get them ready for the opening. We can feature them. But you have to say yes."

"Would I have to hang out with you in Hawai'i?"

"Yes. A luxury hotel is paying for me to go and post on my Instagram. We will have to dine at their restaurants, use their spa, relax on their beach, snorkel, and swim with dolphins."

Her jaw drops. "Dolphins? Abused dolphins in captivity forced to pose for pictures with tourists? I'd rather stick a fork in my eyeball. No, thanks."

I shake my head. She's unlike anyone I have ever met. I wish I were as passionate about something in my life as she is. I once was passionate about something other than making money. "We can get out of the dolphin swimming. I'll switch that activity out."

"But I don't want to spend time with you. I hate you."

Ha. "You don't have to like me for this scenario to work."

"What about sex?"

Now we're talking, baby. Well, at least we are on the same page. I lower my voice to a whisper and lick my lips.

"Babe, sex can definitely be included. In fact, I'll fuck your brains out right now for a preview."

Her cheeks blush. "Not what I meant. I'm not going to have sex with you. If I agree to go to help you with the opening, it will only be because you have agreed to show-case all the dogs in our rescue there on opening day. And we could really use that donation. And the expo is supposed to be incredible. But I won't owe you anything. I'm not going to sleep with you. Ever."

We'll see about that. "Sex is off the table. Is it a deal? Say yes, Yessi." I can't wait to hear her scream my name.

She fidgets and then takes a long exhale, finally shaking her head. "No, Preston. I can't. I would love to go to the pet expo, and we can really use the cash, but it's against everything I believe to work in a puppy store."

Fuck. I thought I had her. I was so close. But I'm still in the fight.

"Fine, I understand." I pause and replay our conversation in my head. "Let me get your number just in case I have a question about the dog. Then I'll drop you off at your car."

We exchange numbers, she bids goodbye to Gidget, and we leave my place. I drop off her in front of her car.

"Night, Yessi. Nice to meet you."

"Good night, Preston."

She scrambles into her car and then drives away from the store.

But I know she's thinking about Hawai'i. She will go with me.

Time to pack.

CHAPTER FIVE

As my car races down the street, I try to process what just happened. Did Preston Evans really invite me to Hawai'i? And even worse, did I just say no?

Of course, I did. I'm a responsible, practical, and rational woman. I don't even know the guy.

Well, actually that's not true.

I hate to admit it, but I know way more then I should know about Preston Evans. I wouldn't say I've stalked him, but I follow him on Instagram. And Snapchat. Images flood my mind of him posing shirtless in Ibiza: his muscles glistening from the salt water, his huge tattooed arms flexing for the camera, his incredibly defined abs shining in the sunlight. Just picturing his body makes me want to drop to my knees and suck his cock.

Speaking of his cock, it is as perfect as its owner. It has been screenshot and posted everywhere. Long, thick, and juicy.

And that video of his? Damn. I'd be lying if I said I haven't watched it. Initially, it was part of some morbid curiosity. His ex, Kira Morgan, is a reality superstar and a stunning celebrity yoga instructor. Despite her star power, Preston definitely stole the show. He's a dirty talker—dominate and delicious. Though the snap was only ten seconds, an extended version leaked on to Pornhub. Usually, I detest porn so, instead, I indulge in erotica. The men in the porn I've watched were always so vile, disrespectful, and self-centered.

But not Preston.

What got me wasn't the voyeuristic aspect. No, it was the *way* he fucked her. It was unlike any other porn I've ever seen. Or any sex I have ever experienced. As cocky as Preston was, he was one hundred percent about Kira. Fully focused on her pleasure. In absolutely no rush at all. He was determined to make her come—which she did, again and again. Hell, I will never admit it to him, but he's already been responsible for one of the most intense orgasms of my life.

And damn, that boy ate her pussy like a champ. But, still, it was more than that. He looked at her like he loved her. And he had just told Gidget's bastard owner that he had loved Kira. The tabloids reported he had dumped her after the release of the video, furious that she had gone behind his back and exploited him. But who knows if that is true?

All I knew was that when I watched his video, I wondered what it would be like to have a man look at me the way Preston looked at her. No one has ever looked at me like that. Jealousy consumed me when I watched him fuck her. I wanted to be Kira.

But I'm nothing like that famewhore.

I grab my phone and dial Avril.

"Hello?"

"Hey. You won't believe what happened to me."

"Oh God, no. What did you do? Did you save another chi?"

"No, no. Not that. I was driving on Main Street, and I saw Doggy Style! Like the lights were gleaming, beckoning people to buy these puppy mill dogs. And I don't know what happened, Avril. I lost it. I pulled my car over and handcuffed myself to the door."

She lets out a laugh. "Good for you. Did you get arrested? Am I your one phone call?"

Wouldn't be the first time. "No. It was even worse."

"What's worse than getting arrested?"

"Meeting Preston Evans."

A squeal radiates through the phone. "Oh my god, shut up girl! Is he even hotter in person? Did you fuck him?"

"What the fuck, Avril? No, I didn't fuck him. We hate him, remember? Just an hour ago you were talking about burning his place down, and now you want to know how hot he is?"

"I didn't say I think he's a good person. But he's literally the hottest man ever. Have you seen his video? Forget his war medals; he should get a medal for fucking."

I shake my head. Avril is always down to fuck. I wish I had her confidence and her game. She could stroll into a bar and walk up to the hottest man and straight up ask him to go home with her while I sit at the bar drinking all night and whining to the bartender.

"Well, to answer your question, yes, he's gorgeous, even hotter in person. He kind of has this Elvis Presley meets Zac Efron vibe going on. But he's an arrogant prick." I pause, still in shock from what I agreed to do. "And get this, he invited me to go to Hawai'i with him tomorrow."

"Shut up! You bitch! Please tell me you said yes. Oh my god, you said no, didn't you? Dammit. Why does this shit never happen to me?"

"Of course, I told him no. He even promised to consider turning Doggy Style into a pet adoption store if I went and worked at his store. And he offered to let us bring all our dogs to the store for the grand opening! And he wanted to donate twenty-five thousand dollars to Pugs N Roses. He's even fostering Gidget, the chi I needed a home for."

"And you said no? Are you high? What the fuck is wrong with you? We need that money. And we need to get our dogs adopted. And he's hot!"

Well, when you put it like that. "I know. I just don't want to owe him anything. And it wasn't just going to Hawai'i. He wanted me to open Doggy Style with him. That means I'd have to sell purebred puppies. I can't do that. It's against everything I believe."

"Listen to me woman. I don't care what you have to do. I don't care if you have to sell puppies at an auction. I don't care if you have to breed the puppies yourself. In order to affect change, sometimes, we have to go out of our comfort zone. In the end, this donation will save so many dogs. And if he stops selling puppies and turns it into an adoption store, we will save even more. This is a once in a lifetime opportunity."

Avril is right. I should've said yes.

"I'll sleep on it tonight."

"Good. I'm just curious why he offered you this opportunity of a lifetime. I mean, you're gorgeous, but he can have any woman in the world. Why would he change his store concept for some psycho girl protesting outside of his shop?"

If anyone else said that to me, I'd be offended. But I understand what Avril meant. "Believe me, I asked him the same thing. He's a huge influencer and also said we would have to take pictures at the hotel. Hell, he wanted me to swim with captive dolphins, but I told him no way in hell. I think he is afraid we will protest and ruin his shop, which we will. And I think he liked that I stood up to him."

She sighs. "Call him tonight and say you will go. I'm so jealous right now. I seriously hate you. You better fuck him like a porn star, so he turns his puppy joint into an adoption center. Pull out all the stops. Deepthroat his delicious cock. Let him do you doggy style. Baby talk to him all breathy. Men love that shit."

I may be selective about who I sleep with, but I definitely didn't need any pointers in bed. I'm a freak. "You're crazy. I'll consider going, but I'm not going to sleep with him." Maybe if I say that three times out loud, I'll finally believe it.

She laughs. "Yeah, right. You've seen his video, right? This is a once in a lifetime opportunity. If you don't do it for yourself, do it for me."

"No. No way. Sex is off the table. His words." But if sex is off the table, why do I want him to bend me over it?

"Whatever, woman. Sex is *never* off the table."

A wave of fear hits me. Was I actually going to agree to go to Hawai'i with a man I didn't know? This is crazy. I'm not the type of woman who jumps into bed with every man I meet. No judgment at all on Avril. In fact, I'm jealous of the way she owns her sexuality, but I can't even consider sleeping with a man unless I have feelings for him. I'm also not even remotely spontaneous. As a card-carrying Capricorn, I plot and plan every detail of my life. I most certainly do not travel to faraway islands with a man I don't know.

But a part of me wants to, not just for the dogs, but for me. Let my hair blow in the wind, inhale the scent of the salty air, bask in the sun, relax in the sand, dip my toes in the ocean, sip a Mai Tai.

And even a bigger part of me wants Preston to do me doggy style.

"Well, we'll see. If I go, I'm going to text you all my flight information and his number just in case he ends up kidnapping me. And I'll need you and Eden to help me bring all the fosters to his store. He offered to also watch my own dogs at the store, but I think I should bring them to you and take your fosters to the store. That way, we have a better chance of getting them adopted."

"Yup, sounds good. I'll be there, and I'll drag Eden. I may try to stow away in your luggage. Anyway, girl, go home and get your rest. You'll need it."

I sigh. "Thanks. Bye."

I hang up and continue driving down the Pacific Coast Highway, my mind replaying my conversation with Preston. Is he a gentleman like he says he is? He was awarded medals for heroism in war. Could he be a hero for millions of dogs? Could he really consider turning his store into an adoption center? If so, he'd no longer be my nemesis.

I walk into my apartment, let the dogs out into my small yard, and dial Preston's number.

"Miss me already?"

What a cocky, arrogant son of a bitch. I throw my hands up in defeat, not that he can see me. "Fine, Preston. I'm in. But I swear to God, if you are lying to me it will be hell to pay. I will have hundreds of rescuers destroy your place. I'm going to give you a chance to do the right thing. Let me be clear—this is an educational trip for me. I'll be the teacher, and you will be my student. After I'm through with you, you will realize how reprehensible it is to own a puppy store. This is not a romantic vacation."

"I'll cancel the romantic couple's massage. And the dolphin excursion. Anything else?"

"No. I'll be at your store on Thursday morning."

We exchange information for the plane ticket.

"I'm excited Yessi. I'll show you a great time."

Yeah, I bet. "I'm sure you will. Don't cancel the massage. I think I'll need it."

He laughs. "Yes, you most definitely will."

CHAPTER SIX

PRESTON

I arrive at the shop at seven on Thursday morning. I couldn't sleep all night imagining what it would be like to fuck Yessi, taste her sweet pussy, hear her scream my name, watch her come all over my cock. How long has it been since I felt this kind of anticipation, this hunger, this desire?

But this woman doesn't even like me. Despite all my Instagram followers, I sometimes wonder if a majority of people look at me as a joke. That would be so ironic because I began my adult life wanting to help people, serving in the Marine Corps because I wanted to fight for our country. And, lately, it seems the only person I have been benefitting is myself.

I walk Gidget into the store. I'm shocked at what a good dog she has been in the two days that I've had her. She's fully house trained and hasn't destroyed my furniture. She also loves to cuddle and watch movies with me, and even brings me her food bowl every day.

I can't believe that she would've been killed if I hadn't saved her.

Hugh shows up, disheveled and hungover. He murmurs something unintelligible when he sees me.

I slap his back. "Dude, pull it together. We open in less next week and because I'll be out of town, I need you to handle everything. Can you help me get these kennels ready for the dogs Yessi's bring in?"

His bloodshot eyes bulge. "Dogs? What the fuck are you talking about?"

"I told you the other night. She runs a dog rescue. She saves dogs from high kill shelters. I told her she could keep the dogs here and we can feature her rescues on opening day. Should be good for publicity."

Hugh gets in my face; a whiff of stale whiskey overtakes me. "Fuck no, Evans. I don't care if you got pussy on your brain. We are a high-end pet store. Purebreds and designer dogs only. We don't want some mangy mutts soiling our brand."

I stare him down. "Non-negotiable. I already told her yes. Besides, stop being such a dick. These dogs were going to die. We can still sell the puppies. I thought this entire concept was about giving our customers' choices."

He shakes his head. "Fine. But don't get any crazy ideas. This is a puppy store, not some charity. We're here to make a profit."

I give him a scowl but hold my tongue. I'm not going to engage him, especially since I'm headed out of town today. This business is Hugh's life—he doesn't have a girl-friend, lives above our new store, and left his job to run Doggy Style. I owe him my gratitude—even if he can be a jerk.

"Are you still pet sitting for me?"

Hugh squints his eyes. "Pet sit? You mean house sit?"

"No, I mean pet sit. I'm fostering this dog for Yessi. She's really sweet and totally housetrained. You won't even know that she is there."

Hugh shakes his head. "Nope, not going to happen. I

agreed to spend a few days at your place overlooking the ocean. I'm not going to take care of some reject dog."

I resist the urge to deck him. I really should, but I can't start a fight with him today. He's usually not this much of a dick. Maybe he's just stressed about the opening of the shop.

"Fine. Then you can't stay at my place. I'll just keep her here."

"Whatever, man."

I place Gidget in one of the cages out front, and head to the back room and prepare to sanitize the kennels. After I've gathered the brush and bucket, I get down on my hands and knees to scrub the floors. The toxicity of the bleach makes my eyes water, and my knuckles begin to bleed.

Hugh follows me into the room. "What the fuck are you doing, dude? We have janitors for that shit."

I glare at him. "Yeah, well, the dogs are coming in now, and this place is a sty. Get your lazy ass over here and help me out."

He shakes his head. "Nah, man. That's on you. You're better than that."

"Fuck you, man. No, I'm not."

Fuck him. My dad taught me that I'm never better than anyone else. Success comes from hard work. I'm not afraid to get dirty and do manual labor. Every breath I take is a blessing. Every day of my life, I'm thankful that I'm alive and that I exited the battlefield in one piece and didn't leave the Middle East in a flag-draped coffin like some of my buddies did.

Like Marquis did.

Hugh storms off like a petulant child. Sometimes, I want to strangle him. But he's an equal investor in this place, a decision I'm questioning now.

I refuse to waste another thought on him. Time to focus on Yessi.

How many dogs did she say she had? Eleven at her place? Hugh is going to kill me. Hell, I don't blame him for being pissed.

After I went home the other night, I studied the website for her rescue, Pugs N Roses. The site was dated and sad, but my heart wrenched when I saw the pictures of the dogs they had saved: pathetic shelter pictures of dogs that had seen better days. Reminded me of the street dogs I saw in Iraq. I want to help get Yessi's dogs adopted. I just don't know who will adopt them when they will be displayed next to our puppies. I see why she's upset about the store.

I blast music and continue preparing the kennels. I place new beds, water, and food bowls in each stall. Just as I toss in the final toy, I hear the puppies yelp loudly. The barking lot has alerted me that my date has arrived.

I walk to the front of the store, and my breath hitches when I see Yessi clutching the leashes of a bunch of scared looking dogs. Her angry scowl from the other night is long gone, replaced by an almost hopeful look. A glimpse of her hot pink bra strap poking out from under her black tank top drives me wild with anticipation. Is she wearing matching panties? Does she have any other hidden tattoos that I can discover? I want to map out every inch of her body.

She's standing in between two other women—a trendy blonde and an earthy redhead. Both of them are beautiful, but I only have eyes for Yessi.

Her own eyes widen when she sees me, and I laugh to myself, realizing that I'm shirtless. I wipe the sweat off my brow.

"Hi, Yessi. Nice to meet you, ladies. I'm Preston. I was just getting the kennels ready."

The blonde checks me out head to toe. "We can see that. Are you done, or can we watch—I mean, help?"

I laugh. "I'm done." I take the leashes of a few dogs and lean into Yessi. "I didn't think you'd show up."

"That makes two of us. But I'm here. These are my rescue partners, Avril and Eden. We are all grateful for this opportunity to get our dogs adopted."

A tiny min pin with a frosty mug and sad eyes pees on the floor in front of me, his tongue darting in and out like some nervous tic.

I grab some paper towels and some dog spray and clean up the mess. This sorry looking dog will definitely need some help getting adopted. I walk over to the row of doggy couture and select out a tuxedo jacket for him, and a pink polka dotted dress for Gidget. I tug the tuxedo jacket on the min pin. He looks much regaler now. Then I remove Gidget from her cage, pet her gently, and slip the dress over her head. She licks my nose.

Eden places her hand over her heart, and Avril pinches Yessi. But Yessi is still not won over by my efforts. Her face remains stoic.

I'm not worried. She will soften to me.

Hugh finally decides to grace these women with his presence. "Not sure what Preston has told you, but this is a one-shot deal. We are a puppy store, not a place for homeless mutts."

I shake my head. I expect more from him. He comes off as such a jerk. I'm shocked he didn't even try to flirt with Avril or Eden.

A scowl appears on Yessi's face. She turns to Avril. "See—I told you Preston isn't going to change the store."

Avril opens her mouth, but I interrupt. "Ignore him. I'm a man of my word. I've set up the kennels for the dogs. Follow me, and we can get everyone situated." I walk ahead of them and look over my shoulder to see Avril whispering something to Yessi, who just rolls her eyes. But once we reach the kennels, I turn around and notice that Yessi's lips are quivering.

"You did this for them? They can actually stay here?"

I beam with pride. "Yup. We have full-time kennel attendants and a vet who will come in once a week to check every dog. Every Friday, all the dogs will also be groomed."

Yessi reaches into her purse and pulls out a manila envelope and a plastic baggie full of medication. "I have every dog's vaccination records and shelter paperwork in the envelope and a list of their daily medications. Most of them are healthy but a few are recovering from kennel cough, and some of them were recently fixed." She turns her head back toward the front of the shop where Hugh is standing. "He's not going to be taking care of the dogs, is he?"

I shake my head. "No. He's my partner and handles the financial aspects of the business. I take care of the social media and marketing. The kennel attendant will be in today, and she will give me updates on all your dogs. He was going to watch my place, but he doesn't want to pet sit Gidget. Do you mind if she stays here?"

"No. That's fine. Gidget probably doesn't want to stay with him either."

Eden escorts each dog into a kennel. "I truly want to thank you for allowing our dogs to be here for the opening. We would love to partner with your store. I really hope you will listen to Yessi and turn this store into a wonderful place for the community to save lives."

I study the dogs in front of me. I'd imagined them all to be mutts, but there were a few purebreds sprinkled in the sea of chihuahuas. A brown dachshund rolled on his back as a fluffy poodle sniffed a beagle's butt. Did this rescue really find all these dogs in shelters? I have to admit: I've never been to an animal shelter. I'd just assumed that it was for old, sick dogs. A pang of guilt hits me hard—am I really doing the wrong thing? Contributing to the slaughter of homeless pets? Will this be my legacy?

"I'm looking forward to having Yessi teach me about shelter dogs." I look at my phone. "We have to head to the airport. Ladies, thank you again. The dogs will be taken care of, and if you need to come into the store for any reason, please text Yessi, and I'll arrange it."

Yessi runs her hands through her hair. "I'll walk you guys out."

Avril hugs me. "Nice to meet you, Preston. Take care of my girl, or you'll have me to answer to."

Charming.

I lean into Yessi. "I'm going to hop in the shower really quick and meet you down here."

Her eyes dance around my body. "Shower?"

"Yeah, Hugh lives above this place. Check out our store. I'll be done in a few minutes."

I race upstairs, strip naked, and jump into the shower. As the hot water beads down my body, I wonder what Yessi's backstory is. Why did she start rescuing dogs? How is she still single? Well, clearly, she has strong opinions and convictions, but I find that attractive in a woman. I'm assuming that if she had a boyfriend, she would've told me last night when I asked her to come with me on a tropical vacation. Why am I so drawn to her?

It isn't love at first sight, no. It is an insatiable lust, a lust I haven't felt in years.

Not since Kira.

But Kira longed for the limelight. And for the first time since I'd become infamous, I desired anonymity.

I towel off, grab my suitcases, and head downstairs. Yessi is crouched down in front of the kennels, petting the min pin through bars.

"You ready? We need to go."

"Yeah. I just feel so guilty leaving Gidget here. She was just dumped by her owner, you took her home one day, and she probably feels abandoned again. She doesn't even know what's going on."

And that's when I saw it. Her heart. Yessi doesn't even

know this dog, but she already loves her. I wonder what it would like to be loved by a woman who cares so much about others.

Lately, I've been so wrapped up in showcasing my image to make this store a success that I've forgotten what it was like to focus on someone other than myself.

Maybe I have become a selfish asshole.

I slowly take Yessi's hand. "She'll be alright. I'll have the vet come to check on her today and take care of any medical expenses she needs."

Her lashes blink open wide. Her eyes hypnotize me. "Thanks for doing this for the dogs—no matter what your motivation is."

"I know you think I'm a jerk, but I can already tell you are a sweet, loving woman. And you have to know how beautiful you are. Give me a chance, Yessi. You take care of all of these dogs all the time—let me take care of you for a week."

"This is the craziest thing I've ever done. But you saved Gidget's life, and you can save so many more." She exhales. "I'm going to try to keep an open mind, but that's all I can promise you. I've always wanted to go to the pet expo, and I really do need a vacation."

That's all I need. A maybe. I have a chance. I lift her hand to my lips and kiss it.

She doesn't flinch. I help her up off the floor, take her luggage, and we climb into the waiting limo. Next stop: paradise.

CHAPTER SEVEN

YESSI

Though my nerves still rattle inside me, I feel calmer than I thought I would feel. I was shocked at how amazing the kennels looked in the store.

And Preston. I was legit drooling when I saw him, standing there shirtless, sweat dripping down his incredible chest. His scent was masculine and woodsy. But I was even more impressed that he himself had been cleaning the kennels. I never pictured someone as seemingly rich and successful as him doing dirty work.

And I couldn't help myself from getting wet when he picked up Gidget and placed her in that dress. Swoon.

As the limo leaves the store, I keep my eyes glued outside the window toward the ocean.

I glance over, and he is checking his phone, a smile on his face. What am I doing here with him? Why did he ask me again? Because I'm a challenge?

But it doesn't matter. No matter how hot he is, I can't get involved with him. Even if he honors his pledge and turns Doggy Style into an adoption store, we are too different. He is a social media magnet—I'm a hermit. He uses Instagram to promote himself, and I use it to save lives.

"So, how long have you been a tattoo artist? I looked at your work on Instagram. You are talented."

I sigh. I don't want to open up to him, but we are about to be trapped in a steel tube for six hours as we fly over the ocean. I can't avoid speaking to him. So, instead, I make a silent vow to be polite, but distant. "Four years. I used to draw all the time when I was younger." *In my foster home.*

"That's cool. Maybe you can give me a new tattoo. I can always use another."

Nope. Not going to happen. He's trying to find a connection with me. I can't risk falling for this guy. It crosses my mind that maybe he invited me as some type of joke or bet, like one of those cheesy romantic comedies where his buddy bet him that he couldn't fuck the deranged, tattooed animal rescuer who was chained to his store.

"Doesn't matter. Look, I appreciate what you are trying to do here, but I'm not interested. You know you are hot. I'm not going to lie and say I'm not attracted to you, but I'm not interested in taking this further. I'm here solely because I need you to stop selling puppies. And I'm grateful that you are letting our dogs be at your store on opening day, but I'd prefer to keep our interactions professional."

He smirks. "Fine, professional it is. Miss Cordova, what would you like to do on our business trip to the Aloha state?"

I glower at him. I still think he is playing me. "I'll go with you to the pet expo as promised. I would like you to attend the rescue summit. And, one day, I'd like to tour the Hawaiian Humane Society with you so you can learn more about animal shelters. I'll agree to have certain meals with you where I can teach you more about animal rescue. But I'd like my evenings off." I packed a book which I was dying to read, *The Shark Dialogues* by Kiana Davenport. It is supposed to be this incredible epic family saga about Hawai'i. Maybe I'll also spend some time sketching. But most importantly, I just want to relax—sleep in without waking up five times a night to give eye drops to my foster dog, disconnect instead of checking my email constantly to get the daily euthanasia lists from the shelters, turn off my phone instead of answering calls from fosters who, at the last minute, change their minds and dump their fosters dogs at my house, have my room cleaned instead of scrubbing my apartment daily due to my failed efforts housebreaking a dog who had spent his entire life outside. A week to try to find peace before I go back to my crazy life.

"Sounds like a plan. Though I have tickets to a concert at a club downtown—my buddy is playing there. I would like you to go with me."

Sounds like a date. "Your buddy? Did you grow up in Hawai'i? Oh wait, you were stationed there, right?" God, I'm such a dork. I'm legit quoting his wiki. He must think I'm so pathetic.

His lips widened into a smile. "I thought you wanted to keep this professional. Where did you grow up?"

Dammit. He's right. Those were my words. And he didn't want the answer to where I grew up. Everywhere. Nowhere. "I do. The club sounds fine." I hate myself right now. I can't even play off the cool, detached vibe. He must know how attracted I am to him. I must try to be more aloof.

Yet, he seems so calm, so cool. Not remotely annoyed by my hesitation or my rules. Patient. Is he really a gentleman like he claims he is?

The limo pulls up at the airport, and he exits from his side. I grab my purse and attempt to open the door. I see the limo driver hop out of the car and come toward me, but instead, Preston opens my door.

"Thank you," I offer.

He walks toward the back of the limo and hoists my luggage out of the trunk. I attempt to take my bag from him, but he resists. "I got it."

Ugh. I'm doomed.

"No. I'll carry it myself." I snatch it from him.

But if I thought his chivalrousness is the most awkward part of this trip, I soon learn I'm dead wrong. A few steps into the terminal and a bright light flashes in my face.

What the hell?

A sexy blonde reporter in a miniskirt shoves a microphone

in Preston's face. "Preston, Preston, is this your new girlfriend?"

Preston puts his arm around me, and I don't push it away. I melt under his firm grip.

"Don't say anything. Just keep your head down and keep walking. They can't harass us once we pass security."

I nod, push my sunglasses over my eyes and, for once, I do as I'm told.

But the lights don't stop flashing. And the questions keep coming.

A man facing us but running backward keeps taking pictures. "What's your name, honey? Are you a porn star?"

What the fuck? Do I look like a fucking porn star? Is this the shit that Preston has to deal with daily?

I'm about to open my big mouth to tell him off when Preston drops his bag and lunges at the guy. Preston grabs the pap by the shirt and slams him to a wall. "Shut the fuck up, man! Apologize to her now, or I'll knock your teeth out."

Whoa. My heart races. I'm so turned on right now. No

one has ever stood up for me. Ever. My ex actually called animal control on me.

I dash over to Preston. "Preston, stop. I'm okay. He's not worth it. Let's go."

The weaselly reporter squeaks. "Listen to your girlfriend, man, just let me go. I won't press charges if you let me get a good shot."

"Not a chance, dude." Preston releases him.

Dammit. I don't want him to get arrested over me. "Let's just let him get his shot."

Preston's head tilts toward me, and my lips ache, wanting to be kissed. I finally pull away from him and smile for the picture.

The paparazzo doesn't hesitate to start snapping pictures. Once the jerk finally stops, we turn away. I grab my bag. Preston gathers his and puts his arm around me again and leads me into security.

"Sorry about that."

I shake my head. "Don't apologize. Wasn't your fault at all. What a jerk. Do you deal with this every day?" It never occurs to me what kind of hell it must be like to live like this.

"Yeah. I mean I was used to it when I was dating Kira and it never really bothered me. She liked it, would stop and pose. The paps loved her. I was just trying to be supportive of her. I was new to LA and this whole scene." He pauses, and his brow furrows. "But once she posted that video, the attention went to a whole new level. I'm just kind of over it, you know?"

"Nothing like that has ever happened to me. I mean, I spend so much time begging on Facebook for pledges, foster homes, transporters, that I have always wanted more exposure. But now I see how invasive it is."

"Yeah. I wonder if I'll ever get back to being anonymous."

He flashes his ID and phone with his boarding pass on it to the TSA guard. I turn my head and notice a few girls in line behind us taking our picture.

Wow.

Ever since I met him, I've imagined that he had no problems in the world—just some cocky, rich jerk who thinks he can buy people, like me.

But now I have a glimpse into the dark side of his reality. And for the first time since he had asked me to go to Hawai'i, I understand why he might be actually interested in me. Not just because he is attracted to me or because I'm a challenge. I'm sure there are elements of that in there. But because when he met me the other night, he saw a girl who clearly didn't care about her appearance. I was wearing dirty jeans and a ratty shirt covered with dog hair. My only care in the world was saving the dogs. A girl who had no desire to live in the limelight that he's tired of.

"Miss, your ID please."

"Oh, right. Sorry."

I flash my ID and boarding pass to the TSA agent. I then proceed to remove my flips flops and deconstruct my carry-on into the bins, carefully separating my three-point-four-ounce bottles of sunscreen, moisturizer, and cleanser.

Preston is a few steps ahead of me, and I do everything within my power not to stare at his incredible ass. But another part of his body catches my attention—his eyes. I notice that he is checking out every single person in the baggage area. Not creepily, no not at all. It's as if he is assessing them. For what, I don't have a clue. But I do know he was a sniper. Is he scanning them for threats? In the security area?

Maybe it's some old habit that's hard to break.

He catches my gaze and winks at me. I can't help but melt.

God, I'm so weak.

"You ready?"

"Yup."

He insists on carrying my bags up the escalator, and this time, instead of fighting him, I hand him my bag without hesitation.

CHAPTER EIGHT

PRESTON

As we sit in the terminal waiting for the boarding agent to announce that it's time to board, I notice a change in Yessi. It's subtle, for sure, but she has definitely softened toward me. She allowed me to carry her bag and now her body is leaning toward me, a lock of her hair resting on my shoulder. I resist the urge to wrap my arm around her and claim her for myself.

I check my phone and see a few messages from Hugh, whining about Yessi's dogs.

Hugh: These nasty ass dogs are taking up space. I can't believe you agreed to this shit.

Preston: Deal with it. About to board. I'll text you when we land.

A lady steps up to the podium. "We are now boarding for Hawaiian Airlines flight fifteen with service to Honolulu. We will begin with boarding passengers in our first-class cabin. Welcome aboard."

I touch Yessi's leg. "Let's go, babe."

Her eyes flip open wide, slaying me with her lashes. "We're in first class? I didn't even check the ticket."

"Yup. It's a long flight. I have a ton of miles."

A real smile graces her face. Warmth fills my chest—it's nice to make someone happy for a change instead of always disappointing everyone. Not just my father, but even my ex. She was always nagging me about being more public, trying to turn me into someone I wasn't. She needs to be with someone who wants that life. Deep down, I'm a simple man.

Yessi and I head down the ramp and once inside the cabin, I place our luggage in the overhead bins, and we take our seats. Typically, sitting in first class, about to embark on a vacation to Hawai'i, calms me down, but this time, instead of fantasizing about relaxing on the beach in

Lanikai, I'm filled with anxiety about my business. What if Yessi is right that all the rescuers are planning to protest every day? What if she won't help me stop them?

As if Yessi senses my uneasiness, she places her delicate hand on my arm. The sensation of her touch emboldens me.

"Thanks for all this. I'm actually really excited. I've never been to Hawai'i. I've always wanted to go." She pauses and her nose crinkles which I find incredibly adorable. "About what I said in the limo, I'm sorry about that. I still want to keep this professional. Nothing against you, but I'm really not interested in dating anyone right now. My life is kind of unstable. But I'm going to try to be less of a bitch. I'm just stressed out and nervous. This is the craziest thing I've ever done. I'm normally not impulsive at all."

The flight attendant interrupts us. "Can I get you something to drink? Mai tai, POG, fruit punch?"

As much as I need a whiskey to take the edge off, POG always reminds me of my childhood. "I'll take the POG."

"What's POG?" Yessi asks me.

"Pineapple, orange, and guava juice. It's good. Try it."

"I'll have that, too."

The stewardess walks away, and I turn my attention to the passengers boarding. I can't help myself from surveying every person on this plane. I'm not sure if it's PTSD or just my training in the Corps, but I always imagine everyone I see as a potential threat. I like to be in control at all times. I hate being trapped on a plane over the ocean completely at the mercy of the pilot, the weather, and the passengers. I don't trust TSA to keep me safe.

A screen drops down in front of us, and a short clip plays of some beautiful Hawaiian girls dancing the Hula to some traditional Hawaiian music. I get it—Hawai'i is nothing more than a tropical vacation to most people, but to me, it will always be my home.

"So, did you grow up in Hawai'i?"

I relax into my seat and feel the warmth of her legs pressed against mine. "Yup. I was born in Washington, but my father got stationed in Hawai'i with the Navy when I was five. I lived there until I was twelve and then he was given orders to Illinois. But I consider Hawai'i my home. I love the food, the culture, the people. I would like to move back one day. When I was in the Marines, I was stationed at K-Bay, which is on my favorite part of the island."

"Wow, that's so cool. I've never even left the state, but I've always wanted to travel."

I can't help myself. "I'll take you wherever you want to go."

She blushes. "Do you always just go full force after what you want? I don't get it. Am I some game to you? This can't all be because I said no to you."

She's right. It's not. But I'm not going to open my heart up to her yet. I'm very clear in my head about what I want. I'm insanely attracted to her, but I'm also fascinated by her. But I realize that I don't know her at all. "You intrigue me. It's been a long time since anyone has surprised me. Most women I meet are so superficial. I'm fascinated by how passionate you are about your rescue." *And you have the most incredible ass I've ever seen.* But I'll keep that to myself.

"Yeah, well, they're probably smarter than me. This is the decade I should be building my career. I'm broke as a joke. I'm sick of struggling. I don't need much for me, but our dogs are so expensive. We just paid nineteen hundred dollars for this sheltie's double luxating patella surgery, and we still owe our vet twelve hundred on our bill. We spend on average of eight hundred dollars a dog, but we adopt each dog out for two fifty, seniors for two hundred.

And there are always more dogs. It never ends—it's so depressing. Sometimes I wonder if I'm even making a difference or if I'm just running around like a hamster in a rat race."

"I can't even believe you are saying that. You saved all those dogs. You are totally making a difference."

She doesn't respond. The plane pulls back from the gate and makes its approach on the runway. Yessi bites her lip, and I can tell she's nervous.

"Have you ever flown?"

"No."

I grab her hand in mine, and she doesn't resist. As the plane takes off, she squeezes my hand. She turns her head toward me, and I meet her gaze. After an intense moment, she looks away.

Once we reach our cruising altitude, we recline our seats. I'm enjoying this forced intimacy. I realize how fucked up my life has been lately. As pathetic as it sounds, I haven't spent this much time with a woman without sleeping with her in at least a few years. "How'd you get into rescue?"

She exhales, and a pained look takes over her beautiful face. "I saw a post on Facebook a few years back with this picture of a pug mix. I lived right near the shelter, and a rescue was asking someone to go pull the dog and take him to their vet. Seemed easy enough. But at the shelter, I saw the face of a bunch of little doggies. There was this one, a Chihuahua. Had the cutest little whiskers." She gulps, and I feel guilty for asking her this question. "Anyway, I pulled the dog I was supposed to get and brought him to the vet. But I couldn't forget about the chi. The next day, I found out that he had killed him." She looks out the window toward the clouds. "And I'll never forget his little face. I could've saved him, but I did nothing. That's how I started. And now, I can't quit. It's like the mafia, except we're all broke and our fur coats are made of dog hair."

A lump grows in my throat. I had no idea how bad the local shelters were. Hugh had told me he had done a ton of research and they only killed sick and unadoptable dogs, and I'd trusted him. I was focused more on marketing and branding.

I should've paid more attention to where we found our dogs. The dogs we have received from the breeder seem to be healthy.

But I never saw their mothers.

"I'm sorry. I had no idea how bad the shelters are. But you

know you can always offer your dogs up for adoption at our store."

She raises her voice and narrows her eyes at me. "I appreciate that, but that's not enough. You have to stop selling puppies. Our dogs can't compete with yours. Your store could be this amazing shelter dog rescue center. You can save so many dogs."

"Sounds like a plan." But even though I believe those words and have good intentions behind them, I knew that I was up for a fight with Hugh. I had made Yessi a promise in the spur of the moment—my cock making promises that I couldn't keep.

My words seem to cheer her up. Her face glows, but guilt crashes over me.

Would I be able to keep the business sustainable if we just adopted out rescue dogs instead of selling purebreds? I could sell a purebred Goldendoodle for three thousand dollars. Adopting out a dog for two hundred and fifty dollars definitely wouldn't pay the bills.

But I still have a week to figure it out. Get some more information from her and present it to Hugh. Deep down, he's a good guy. He should do the right thing.

She excuses herself to use the bathroom, and I think about

how much I would love to finally indulge in my fantasy of joining the mile-high club.

Maybe I'll get to on our flight home.

She returns to her seat a few minutes later and smiles up at me. "Do you mind if I take a nap? I'm so exhausted. I was up all night with the dogs trying to get all their stuff together, and packing."

"Not at all. It's a long flight. Make yourself comfortable."

She props a pillow up on the window, curls her tight little body up into a ball and closes her eyes. Within five minutes, she's out cold, her breath coming in and out in a slow beat. I'm dying to rub her sexy little feet, make her moan with ecstasy.

But she's made it clear that she doesn't want to date me. Even worse, she admitted that she was attracted to me. Her desire for me won't outweigh her rationality. She doesn't seem to be the type of girl to get swept up in romance.

Only one thing I can do.

Make her see that I'm more than the jerk with the sex tape.

CHAPTER NINE

YESSI

Fear takes over my mind as our plane approaches landing. I reach over and grip Preston's hand against my better judgment. He smiles and calmly squeezes my hand back, his touch warm and reassuring.

I gaze out the plane's window and marvel at the breathtaking tropical island that is slowly coming into view. The ocean is clear, deep, and bright and the lush foliage paints a stunning landscape.

For a moment, anxiety fills my chest, and I ponder the possibility of our plane plummeting into the ocean. Clearly, I've binge-watched *LOST*, my favorite television series, one too many times. I've always identified with Kate. She had a rough upbringing, just like me. Though she had a hard shell on the outside, she was vulnerable deep down.

When our plane finally touches down, I exhale. I drop Preston's hand and wait for the plane to pull into the gate.

But even though we are safe on land, my nerves are still on high alert. I am now trapped on an island with a man I don't even know.

Preston stands up and retrieves my bag from the overhead storage. "Ready to go, babe?"

I wince when he calls me babe, but don't call him out on it. For some reason, I don't feel like he is trying to be disrespectful. I vow to just roll with it. "Yup."

We disembark from the plane and gather the rest of our luggage from baggage claim. A short man dressed in a tuxedo greets us with a sign with Preston's name on it, and the man places a lei around my neck. The fragrant scent of plumeria tickles my nostrils, and for the first time since I agreed to go with Preston, I don't regret my decision. In fact, I start to look forward to this trip.

The driver leads us to a limo parked in the terminal. I immediately grab my phone and text Avril.

Yessi: Hey. Just landed.

Avril: Did you join the mile-high club? Are you drunk on Mai Tais?

I laugh.

Yessi: Nope, but I had some pretty strong POG. I'll text you when we check into the hotel.

As the limousine pulls out of the terminal, relief washed over me, and it's not just from the humid air. I'm on vacation—I'm actually in Hawai'i, a place I never thought I'd be able to visit. And Preston has made this dream, one I once thought of as impossible, come true.

The silence between Preston and me is awkward, and, at this moment, I attempt to open up my heart. If this guy is knocking himself out to try to impress me, the least thing I can do is give him a chance. Still, I question his motivations.

I move closer to him in the backseat and allow myself to really look at him. His incredible muscles are visible underneath his shirt, and the bottom of a tattoo peeks out from his sleeve. Since I've already seen him naked in his video, I know precisely what that tattoo is—an eagle, globe, and anchor against the backdrop of an American flag. I also know that he is seriously packing a huge cock under his shorts, but I try not to think about it, and focus instead on the tattoo.

"Who did the ink?"

He pulls up his sleeve, and I pretend like I've never seen the tattoo before, even though I've drooled over him shirtless in his store earlier today. "Actually, a place down here in Honolulu. The guy is excellent. You have some pretty badass ink yourself."

"Thanks. I designed this one myself," I say, pointing to the *Catrina* on my arm. "That's the kind of work I do. I've been getting into watercolor tattoos lately."

"It's beautiful. You are really talented."

His phone beeps, and he looks down. I watch as his eyes scan the screen and then he throws down his phone and then clenches his fist. He quickly turns his head and looks out the window.

"What's wrong?"

He just shakes his head.

I don't know what to do. I haven't been sweet to him at all, even though he has shown me nothing but kindness. But I recognize the look of pain on his face as one I know intimately. He has just received some bad news.

I place my hand on his thigh. "Hey, I'm sorry I've been cold. I'm just a mess, but I'm a really great listener. What happened?"

He places his own hand over mine, and my heart rate accelerates. "My dad."

A lump gathers in my throat. "Is he okay?"

"Yup, he's fine. He just hates me."

Damn. "I'm so sorry, Preston, that's awful." I'm not going to lie and tell him that I relate because I can't. No one ever cared enough about me to hate me. In a way, sometimes, I think it's better that I have never loved or been loved at all.

Not by any humans at least.

The limousine passes by a beautiful beach, but I'm focused on Preston. "Why does he hate you?"

He grits his teeth. "He hasn't spoken to me since that tape was released. He thinks I leaked it on purpose to become famous."

"But you didn't, right?"

"Right. Kira denies leaking it, but I don't believe her. Who else would've done it? I mean, she's always wanted to be the next Kim Kardashian."

I roll my eyes. "Well, that's one way to do it."

"I know. That sounds bad, but she isn't horrible. She's a wonderful woman. We just weren't right for each other."

I'm impressed that he isn't bad mouthing his ex like most men I've met do. "Why?"

"She just wanted a different life than I wanted. She wants to be super famous and get her own reality show. It was out of control. She won't be happy until she's queen."

Wow. "Judging by your Instagram, I thought you wanted to be famous, too. I mean, why would you date someone who was in the public eye if you didn't want to be in it?"

"It wasn't like that at all. I didn't know who the fuck she was when I met her. I'd been deployed in Iraq and don't watch much television. I came back, and she was teaching yoga for vets with PTSD. I just thought she was hot. I didn't know that she had been on a reality show. She was really great to me. She helped me through some really tough times. I loved her. But I just want a simple life. No drama. Financial success from hard work. A passionate relationship that's just for my partner and me, not for the world to see."

I hang on the word simple. My life has always been anything but simple. Chaotic, loud, busy, uncertain, and heartbreaking. Definitely not simple. "That sounds like bliss."

He smiles at me. "Bliss? I think so. But most girls don't. You are nothing like the type of girls I date. Don't get me wrong—you're beautiful, of course, but you don't seem to be remotely impressed by my money."

"I'm impressed with your work ethic—and that you saved your men overseas—but I also think you care more about the bottom line than about doing what's right. Clearly, you're hot, but your looks don't blind me to your faults." Well, that's kind of a lie. He's so sexy I have to look away from him to stop drooling, but he doesn't need to know that.

"My father would like you, Yessi. I barely know you, but you remind me of him. You are passionate and intelligent and not afraid to stand up for what you believe in."

"Does he live here?"

"Yup. But it doesn't matter. He won't see me. I thought . . ." Preston doesn't finish his sentence and looks toward the ocean.

An ache grips my chest—my father didn't want to see me either. Not now, not ever.

I turn toward Preston, but his head is still angled out the window. I touch his cheek and force him to look at me. "You should see him. I'll go with you."

He tilts his head toward me, and for a moment I think he's going to kiss me. Our breaths mingle in the air, and my heartbeat accelerates. I lick my lower lip in anticipation. Preston Evans is going to kiss me and, more importantly, I want him to.

But instead, his lips land on my cheek. "Thanks, babe. Maybe tomorrow. Let's just check into the hotel. I booked you a separate room."

Disappointment fills my chest. While I'm relieved that he booked me a separate room because it shows that he doesn't expect anything from me, I'm silently sad that he might not actually like me. God, I've been so stupid. Of course, he isn't interested in me. He needs me to help him with his store when we get back by getting all the protestors to leave him alone, and he wants to make amends with his dad here in Hawai'i. By chaining myself to his store, I was just in the right place at the right time. I knew he is too good to be true.

He is too hot, too much of a gentleman, too perfect. No guy actually acts like this unless he wants something. I stop believing his whole thing about wanting a simple life. I'm sure that was just a line as well.

I lower my window, and I let go of my reluctant hope that a guy like Preston could ever truly fall for me to blow away in the cool Hawaiian breeze.

CHAPTER TEN

PRESTON

Our limo turns towards the hotel, down a street lined with palm trees. My chest aches and I try to brush away my disappointment from my father refusing to see me. Why won't he believe me that I didn't purposely leak that tape? I've told him the truth many times. Ever since that tape was released, I've pleaded with him to forgive me to no avail.

Kind of how I'm knocking myself out to impress Yessi. She has softened a bit toward me, but she still doesn't seem to like me. Why am I so into her? Is it just the challenge? Strangely, I feel like if I can prove to her that I'm a good guy, then I will be able to prove my honor to my dad as well.

Man, I sound like a fucking pussy.

The hotel comes into sight, and I start fantasizing about spending some time with Yessi tonight. Maybe she will loosen up with a few rum-laden Lava Flows under her belt. Before I can even imagine her naked, the limo shrieks to a halt.

"Damn dog," the driver yells as a stray limps down the street.

Ah fuck.

"Dog?" Yessi asks. "What dog?"

"Just some Poi dog," he says nonchalantly.

She encroaches on his seat. "What's a poi dog? Is he hurt? Where did he go?"

Yup. The dog police is sitting right next to me. So much for my romantic getaway. "A poi dog is a stray dog. He just ran off down that alley."

Yessi's eyes bug out. "There's just some stray dog running around? Did you hit him with the limo? Stop the car." She turns to me and touches my shoulders. "We have to find him. He could be hurt. Or lost."

I quickly realize there is no way Yessi is going to give up until she finds the dog. "Sir, can you let us off here? Just drop our bags off at the Kahala under my name."

The limo driver turns his head as if I just asked him to drive off a cliff. "You are going to chase after some feral dog? Relax. Check into the Kahala. Enjoy your vacation. Forget about that mutt."

Yessi explodes. "I love mutts! Every dog has a soul and deserves love. Stop this car at once."

He slams on his breaks. I slap a hundred into the guy's hand, confirm my name for the reservation, and chase after Yessi, who has already opened the door and left the limo.

"Yessi, wait," I say as I'm running down the sidewalk.

But she doesn't wait. She's wandering in and out of traffic, peering into alleyways, searching for the dog. We make our way to a sidewalk, and she jumps up and down, trying to look over the cars.

"Did you get a look at him?"

I shake my head. "Barely. He's a big dog. Dingy white coat and pretty skinny." I hold her in my arms. "I'm sure someone else found him. Let's just get to the hotel."

She squirms out of my grip. "Don't you get it? That poor dog is out here alone and scared, and you just want to start your vacation. Fuck you, Preston. You can go to the hotel without me."

Tears well in her eyes. Why is saving every dog so important to her?

"I'm not going to leave you here alone. Let's go find the dog."

I grab her hand and start running up the sidewalk, back to where our limo first stopped when the dog ran past. Drivers are honking, and smog cloaks the tropical air.

My eyes search the streets, the sidewalk, the alleys for a dog. For a moment, I'm brought back to Iraq. The hazy air and the smell of exhaust confuse me, and instead of scouring the landscape for a stray, I'm scanning it for insurgents. My fingers shake, and my breath comes in spurts. Sweat drips from my forehead, and I begin to lose touch with reality. Mortars whistle and gunshots ring in my head. I try to shake myself out of it, but I'm frozen in time.

Yessi's voice pierces through my flashback. "I found him!"

I shake myself off, wipe the sweat from my brow, and run over to her, grateful that she was so focused on finding the dog that she didn't witness my PTSD episode. It would be another reason for her to be afraid of me. The real me.

I find Yessi curled up in the alleyway, cornering a sad looking pit bull.

I take a moment and inhale a deep breath and try to remember the man I was back in Iraq. A man who would gladly lay down his life for his country, and I feel a pang in my chest.

I'm no longer that man. What happened to him?

Yessi cautiously starts to walk closer to the dog who is filthy with a raw-looking tail. I notice some blood on his ribs, and he is holding his paw up. I wonder if he was hit by a car.

I put my hand out to stop Yessi from touching him. "What are you doing? You don't know that dog. He could be vicious."

She laughs at me. "Are you afraid of some dog, Preston? He is obviously hurt."

"No, I'm not afraid of him, but he could attack you. We should call animal control and let them deal with it."

She shoots me an angry look. "Fuck you, Preston. Are you insane? In case you can't tell because you don't know shit about dogs, he's a pit bull. And he's injured. Animal control will murder him. We need to take him to the vet.

If he's not chipped, then we can get him healthy and ship him home with us, and I can take him into the rescue. He's skinny and obviously neglected. I'm sure he's a stray."

There's no use arguing with her. "We don't have a leash or a cage or a car for that matter. How exactly do you think we are going to get him to the vet?"

"He's backed into an alleyway. I don't think he will dart pass me if I don't go too close. Go buy a hamburger and a dog collar and leash. I'll wait with him here. We passed a dog store a few blocks back."

Unbelievable.

"Fine, I'll be right back. Call me if anything happens."

"We will be fine."

I run up the sidewalk searching for a store. The Hawaiian humidity drenches my shirt. Well, at least Yessi doesn't seem to care whether or not I look Instagram worthy. Not many girls would spend their first moments of vacation trying to save a stray. And every girl I've dated since Kira has immediately taken a picture of me to post on Instagram. Not Yessi. Maybe she's embarrassed by me.

I finally reach the pet store and buy a large collar, a

leash, and a water bowl. Once I pay, I stop at McDonald's and buy a plain cheeseburger and two bottles of water.

I finally make it back to the alleyway. My jaw drops when I see Yessi petting the pit bull, who is now nestled in her lap.

Lucky dog—I wish my head were between Yessi's thighs. "Wow, you truly are the dog whisperer."

"He's a sweetie. But he isn't fixed. His ears are smelly also, and I think he has some type of skin condition."

She can diagnose dogs, too. I give the dog the hamburger which he gobbles up. I can see his ribs, and my throat tightens. A wave of guilt washes over me.

I finally understand why Yessi is so angry with my store. Like Yessi said, this poor neglected dog would be killed immediately by the shelter. Just like my foster dog, Gidget would be. Everyone wants cute puppies, like the ones I'm selling.

And every time someone buys one of the dogs in my store, a dog like this pit bull dies.

I kneel to the dog and put on his collar and leash. He doesn't resist and, instead, gives me a sloppy kiss.

Yessi smiles and her chest heaves under her shirt. "He's so lucky we found him."

She leans in closer to me, and I breathe her in. She smells spicy yet sweet. I imagine sucking on her nipples, watching her hair cascade down her chest, making her come.

I brush the hair back from her face. "And I'm so lucky that I found you."

CHAPTER ELEVEN

YESSI

Preston hails a cab as I pet the sweet pittie. "It's okay. You're safe now. I got you."

The pittie allows me to pet him, show him love, and ease his pain. I stare deep into his eyes, and we share a moment.

This dog knows that I have just saved his life.

A taxi cab pulls up. The driver takes one look at the dog and drives away. Well, that went well.

Let's try this again.

I stand up and wave down another taxi. Luckily, this one stops and lets the dog and us inside.

"Where to?"

"The nearest vet."

The driver gives me a blank stare. "Where to, lady?"

Uh. I grab my phone and start to search for a vet, but Preston beats me to the punch. "Aloha Animal Hospital."

"Thanks." I appreciate him taking charge and helping me. I snuggle up next to him, and he puts his arm around my shoulders.

"Don't mention it."

The taxi drives through traffic, and I marvel at this day. I'm in Hawai'i on my first vacation in practically forever. Not even ten minutes into our trip, I find a stray dog.

I must be cursed.

Or maybe I'm blessed. "I'm sorry to ruin your vacation."

"It's fine. Who knows what would've happened to him?"

"Uh, me. He would've been caught on a pole by the dog catcher, help at the shelter for three days, and then held down by five people as they murdered him." I close my eyes and try to force the images of shelters dogs waiting in line for their death, being killed for the crime of being homeless out of my mind."

Preston puts his hand on my thigh. "I can't imagine. Well,

now he will be fine. And we still have a few days here so let's try to enjoy it."

I push those depressing thoughts out of my head and try to replace them with fantasies about this trip. I start to get excited, really excited about our vacation. What's going to happen? Are we just going to go to the expo and not spend any time together? Are we going to walk on the beach, sunbathe, go snorkeling?

And more importantly . . . is Preston going to kiss me?

"Here we are." Preston pays the driver, and we get out of the taxi.

We walk into the vet with the dog dragging behind us. He seems sweet, but he's obviously scared and will definitely need a strong handler.

Someone like Preston.

The lady at the front desk stares at the dog. "Do you have an appointment?"

I shake my head. "No. Actually, we just found this dog on the street. Can you scan for a chip?"

The lady nods and grabs the scanner. I hold the dog still, and she scans him head to toe.

No shock, there is no chip.

She picks up the phone. "I'm going to call animal control."

Panic takes over me. "No. Wait. Please don't call animal control. He's clearly a stray and malnourished, and he needs medical care. He was possibly hit by a car. They will kill him for sure. I can pay for his care," I lie. I know for a fact that the rescue card is maxed out, but I can do a fundraiser.

The lady looks at his battered tail and lame gait. "I'll be right back."

She goes into the back room, and I pull at my hair.

Preston leans over to me and whispers into my ear. "Don't worry. I got this. I'll pay for everything."

His hand caresses my cheek, and I can feel the heat of his minty breath on my neck. I close my eyes, desperate to feel his lips on mine, to have him claim me. His lips brush mine and just when I'm certain he is about to kiss me, the lady comes back to the front desk accompanied by a man who I assume is the vet.

Dammit. I could almost taste Preston.

"Hey. You found a dog?" The vet seems friendly, and I'm digging his Hawaiian accent.

"Yup. We are pretty sure he's a stray."

The vet looks him over quickly. "Yeah, he's in bad shape. Looks like a laceration. I agree he was probably hit by a car. Animal control would just put him down. I can do an exam, but we will need to do x-rays and an ultrasound, plus blood work and a fecal." He pauses and stares at Preston and me. "But you would have to take complete ownership and responsibility for this dog. Are you okay with that?"

Preston doesn't hesitate. "Yup. Whatever the dog needs. I mean he'd be dead now, either hit by a car or killed at the shelter, so, let's just get him healthy."

I'm seriously so wet right now. Preston is legit using rescue speak. I clearly don't know my own power.

"Sounds good. Are you local?"

"I used to live here. We both live in SoCal now, but I'll make sure to do right by this dog and then arrange trans- port off the island for him."

"Okay. I need you to fill out some forms, and I'll have Kiana do an estimate." The vet leans down to the dog and pets the dog. "Okay, buddy. This is your lucky day."

The vet takes the dog back into a room as the lady sits at

the desk and starts typing something.

I open my mouth to thank Preston for saving this dog, for fostering Gidget, for taking me to Hawai'i, for everything he has done for me since we meet, but before I can speak, he pulls me to him. His hands cup my face, and his lips press onto mine. The noise from the vet hospital melts away as I breathe him in. His tongue darts into my mouth and I melt into him. I kiss him back, forgetting our unromantic location as I focus on Preston. It's just us alone in this moment, and I never want it to end.

He pulls away, and my heart flutters. I now notice the lady staring at us, and I feel heat flush over my cheeks.

"What's his name?"

My eyebrow cocks, "His? It's Preston."

The lady shakes her head. "No, the dog's name."

Duh. Of course, she meant the dog. I'm such an idiot, but I can only think of Preston. How he tasted. How he felt. And when he will kiss me again.

"Cuffs," Preston says.

I crinkle my face. "Cuffs?"

"Yup. Because that's how we met."

CHAPTER TWELVE

PRESTON

The taste of Yessi still burns on my lips. I can't wait to get her to the hotel room. Cuffs has to stay at the clinic for treatment, but the doctor hopes the dog will make a full recovery. After I arrange for payment to the vet, Yessi and I hightail it out of there.

I call for a taxi. As we wait for it to arrive, I press Yessi into the side of the building and kiss her like I have just returned from deployment. I had never had a girlfriend while I was overseas. I used to be jealous of the men who came home to a loving wife waiting for them when our carrier rolled into the port. Some of the wives would hold up signs that read, "I love my Marine." Those lucky devil dogs would run off the carrier first, sweep their women into their arms, and kiss them like there was no tomorrow.

And I would go home alone and get on a dating app to get laid.

I bite Yessi's lower lip after another passionate kiss. "You are so incredibly hot. I've wanted to do that to you since the moment I saw you."

She kisses me back and rubs her hands over my biceps. "I wanted you, too, even though I couldn't stand you. You're still on probation until you stop selling puppies."

I laugh and kiss her again. I grip her incredible ass.

The taxi pulls up, and we hop into the back seat and neck like teenagers at a drive in. I don't know what it is about Yessi, but I can't get enough of her. She isn't passively receiving my kisses, either. She's aggressively kissing me back. Just days ago, we were mortal enemies, and now, I hope we are about to become lovers.

We finally arrive at the hotel. I breathe a sigh of relief that our limo driver actually took our bags to the hotel when I see them at the valet stand. We step into the breathtaking lobby, and I marvel at the million-dollar view of the ocean outside. I need to come back to this island, my home, regularly, especially when the world gets insane and I lose my way. Hawai'i has always had a way of recalibrating me.

The front desk attendant calls me over to check in. I walk

over to him with Yessi by my side.

"Aloha, Preston Evans. Welcome to the Kahala. Thank you for staying with us. I have reservations for two rooms."

Yessi whispers in my ear, "Cancel mine."

Yeah, baby.

"We will only be needing one room. Could I upgrade to one of your suites?"

"Of course, sir. We have the Kahala Beach Suite available. It is steps away from the sand."

Fuck yeah. Maybe we can go skinny dipping in the ocean. "That would be wonderful. We'll take it."

"Of course, sir. Would you like the bellman to bring up your bags?"

No, because I plan to throw Yessi against the wall and fuck her the second I get to the room.

"No, thanks. I got them."

I tip the bellman for keeping our bags and grab them from the luggage cart.

Once inside the elevator, I kiss Yessi again, pressing my hard cock between her thighs. I want to fuck her right there in the elevator, but once I spy the camera in the corner, I decide that doing that would be an absolutely terrible idea.

I have no desire to make yet another sex tape. I want to keep Yessi to myself.

The elevator arrives on our floor, and after I struggle with the stupid key card, the door opens. I don't even stop to admire the opulence of our suite, the view of the sparkling ocean, or the pristine beauty of the sand. The only beauty I'm interested in appreciating is Yessi.

I pick her up, carry her into the bedroom, and place her on the bed.

I pause to truly appreciate her beauty. She renders me speechless. Her body is perfection—ample breasts, a tiny waist, and a big ol' ass.

Her long eyelashes flip up, and I stare into her eyes which are the hue of rich cognac. She has already shed the sweatshirt she was wearing on the plane, and she's clad in a tight black tank-top and dark jeans. Glimpses of her tattoos are visible at the edge of her clothes. I can't wait to discover every inch of her body.

I lean over her and pull her tank top off over her head. Her skin is tan and flawless, covered only by skin art. Hell, she's a work of art. Her incredible body is adorned with intricate ink. She has some seriously kick-ass tattoos, not the usual girly ones. Her's are fierce, fascinating, and feminine,

Just like her.

I trace the ink on her body down to her hip. Her chest rises when I touch her, and she exhales when I settle myself between her thighs. I'm dying to sink my cock into her, but I'm in no rush.

I turn my attention back to her chest. I can't wait to see her ripe nipples under her bra and to suck on her tits, but I want to tease her first.

I haven't felt this kind of anticipation or hunger for a woman since I'd broken up with my ex. My sex life post break-up has consisted of meaningless swipes through dating apps and shopping from an endless catalog of women. As horrible as it sounds, I don't even remember most of them.

Meaningless sex and hookups soothed my soul for a while. But not anymore. Falling in love with Kira had made me realized that I wanted more than just sex, but once our sex life was exposed, I felt like I lost Kira to the world. I felt betrayed. I didn't trust her anymore.

I want Yessi to be only mine. I refuse to share her.

If she's seen my tape, I'm sure she expects me to be fast and rough, but not tonight. I want to take my time and live in this moment, in this paradise, in her.

I cup her face, close my eyes, and kiss her sweet lips.

We kiss tenderly, gently, slowly, learning each other's mouths, tasting each other, building anticipation for what's to come.

She bites the bottom of my lip, and I growl like one of her dogs.

I unhook her black lace bra and free her beautiful tits when I suddenly become distracted by something metallic on her nipples.

Holy fuck. She has a nipple ring. It's so fucking hot. I've never fucked a woman with a nipple ring before. The shock value alone makes my cock even harder than I thought was possible.

"Jesus, Yessi. Your nipple ring is so hot. You're full of surprises, aren't you? Anything else you are hiding?"

"Undress me and find out."

Yes, ma'am.

How did I not know she had a nipple ring? I've been staring at her tits from the second that I laid eyes on her. The ring is like a hidden treasure meant only for my eyes, like the pearl in the center of an oyster.

I can't wait to suck on her. I lower my lips and take her nipple into my mouth, flicking the ring with my tongue. She gasps and starts to writhe under me. My hand laces with hers and I continue to suck on her. The metallic taste of the ring blends with the sweetness of her flesh. Her hands grip my back as I take her nipple with my teeth.

I focus on her other breast and appreciate the contrast between them. She's just as sensitive and reactive on this nipple. "Do you like when I suck on your nipple? Are you going to come for me, my naughty girl?"

"Presssss."

Her breath comes in waves, and I think she might come just from nipple play alone, but I want her to come in my mouth. I want to taste her pussy and lap up her sweetness.

I force myself to detach from her breast and start to make my way down her body, tracing every line of ink down to her belly button, which is surprisingly not pierced.

I kiss over the waistband of her jeans and marvel at her

curves. Her waist is so tiny, but her hips are wide. She has the perfect hourglass shape.

She props herself up on her shoulders and kisses me again, a hungry kiss. Her hands reach under my shirt, feeling my abs, sending a jolt to my cock. She lifts the shirt over my head and licks her lips when she sees my naked chest.

She climbs on top of me and begins to kiss my body. Her lips are so soft against my hard skin. I've felt desired by other women, but it usually felt like they were interested in me for just a physical connection, and, of course, I feel that way with Yessi, but it's more than that. Seeing her excitement exploring my body and the hunger in her eyes, I feel accepted. Opening a puppy store selling purebreds was definitely a mistake, one I realized this week after meeting Gidget and Cuffs. Most woman would never give me a chance after that error, believing that a man can never change.

But Yessi is here with me now. Sure, I bribed her to come, but she is willing to teach me. Willing to heal me. Willing to save me. Willing to teach me how to be a better man.

Like she has seen my fatal flaw of greed, and she still hasn't run away.

Like Kira did. Like my dad did.

The thought of being accepted as I am, not just as some sex stud, sends fire through my veins.

I refuse to wait any longer.

I need to taste her now.

I pull off her pants and am thrilled when I find out she is wearing a black thong underneath. I flip her over on her stomach to examine her incredible ass. Though I love her breasts, I'm most definitely an ass man, and Yessi's is one for the books.

I squeeze her cheeks and kiss her down the swell of her back. I think of all the things I can do to her ass—spank it, eat it, fuck it, but not tonight.

Tonight, I just want her pussy.

I remove her panties and then flip her over onto her back. I gasp when I see her pussy. It is perfection—a triangle of nicely trimmed dark curls that I can't wait to bury my face into. Unlike many women in So Cal, she is not afraid of her natural hair, her womanliness.

I spread her legs wide and kiss around her thighs, on the top of her lips, all while inhaling her sweet scent. Finally, when I'm unable to resist anymore, I feast on her pussy like I'm a man breaking a fast. Her body immediately reacts to my efforts as she begins to moan, a sweet, breathy moan that causes my cock to harden so much it hurts. Her pussy is everything.

I drown myself in her wetness. She tastes like hot sweet sex, and I'm drunk on her. I press my tongue firmly against her clit, and she gasps. "That's my girl. I want you to come all over my face."

"Ay!"

I discover what she likes as I eat her for all I'm worth. I can tell she's getting close to the edge as her hands clasp my hair, holding me onto her pussy. Her body tenses up and then she explodes as I lap up every last drop of her sweetness.

She giggles like a school girl as I take a final lick.

I pull myself up next to her. Her eyes drop to my cock. "My turn."

"Fuck yeah, baby. You want to suck it?"

"I can't wait."

I sit up on the bed as she crawls over me. She grabs the base of my cock as her lips begin to kiss the tip.

I can feel the moisture from her mouth, but she seems

content teasing me. She rubs her hands up and down my cock, her lips still planting kisses on the tip.

I want to feel her hot mouth around me.

She finally licks under the tip, a sensation that drives me insane. Her mouth opens wide, and I almost expect her to just suck me in a lightly, but I'm pleasantly surprised. Her eyes meet mine and then she deep throats my cock.

Whoa.

Her lips make a perfect seal around me as she sucks me deep. Hard, so hard. I want to explode in her mouth so badly, but I have to pace myself. I want to fuck her tonight.

But her pressure doesn't let up. Her head bobs up and down as her hand rubs along with the rhythm. The difference between the friction of her hand and her mouth drives me wild. I've never had a blow job like this.

She keeps looking up at me and making eye contact. Her eyes slay me and seem to have some type of hypnotic effect over me. Every time she opens those wide eyelashes, I melt inside.

Her lips release their seal around my cock. "Come in my mouth, baby. I want to taste your cum."

What? Most girls never want me to come in their mouths.

"Make me."

Her lips spread into a slick smile, and she starts working my cock with her mouth, with her hand, and her lips. The pressure builds in my balls, and I just want to live in this moment of ecstasy. Her hand clamps tight a final time around my cock, and I explode into her mouth.

I expect her to run to the bathroom and spit out my cum, but instead, she just gives me a satisfied smile and grace-fully swallows.

Damn, this chick is fantastic.

I pull her up to me, and we share a kiss, which is another first for me. So many women won't kiss after oral sex, but I think it's hot and clearly, Yessi does too.

I stroke her hair. "That was incredible."

"I thought so too."

I collapse back onto the bed with Yessi in my arms. I'm not even a little disappointed that I didn't fuck her.

I have the rest of my life for that.

CHAPTER THIRTEEN

YESSI

I awake the next morning tangled up in the sheets. I had slept better than I had in years. Fully satisfied, happy, and, for once, hopeful for the future. I sneak out of bed, slip on Preston's t-shirt and my panties, and open the door to the lānai. I'm grateful for the time change because I woke up naturally in time to catch the Honolulu sunrise.

And what a breathtaking view. The sun rises in the distance, perfectly positioned between two mountains and framed by palm trees. The rays of light from the sun combine with the hues in the ocean to create the most blissful backdrop. Nature's glorious painting. I'm not religious, but if this sunrise isn't proof of a higher power, then I'm not sure what is.

Never in my life have I ever seen anything so beautiful or been anywhere this exciting. Romantic getaways with a generous lover don't happen for girls like me. Poor girls, girls who grew up without a home, girls who grew up without a family, girls who grew up without any love. For some women, a trip to Hawai'i is an annual occurrence or something to take for granted, but for me, witnessing a sunrise in Hawai'i is one of the best things that has ever happened in my life.

I close my eyes and remember all the sexy details of last night. I can't believe I hooked up with Preston. I mean, I guess it was inevitable. Don't get me wrong, I wanted to. I didn't feel pressured at all, but I had vowed before I came to Hawai'i that I would under no circumstance fuck Preston. I didn't want to be distracted from the real purpose of this trip—to go to the expo to learn more ways to save dogs and to convince Preston to stop selling puppies. Now that I have been intimate with Preston, I just want more of him. I can't wait for him to fuck me hard like he had fucked Kira. I want him to do me doggy style.

I have to stop thinking about his incredible cock. Yes, I'm sleeping with the enemy, but no matter how hot he is, or how amazing he is in bed, I will not be distracted from my mission.

I shake those thoughts off. Instead of stressing about things I can't control, I want to live in this moment. Just be present and be here now. For once, I don't want to focus on things I can't change about the past or what I can't predict about the unknown future.

After a few moments enjoying this bliss, I sense Preston's presence. I turn and take in the other breathtaking view—him. He's standing in front of me wearing no shirt and just pajama bottoms. My heart beats rapidly. He's perfection. He sports a six pack and a beautiful happy trail that leads down to his incredible cock. It takes every ounce of control I have to not drop to my knees and suck him off.

"Good morning, beautiful." He gives me a kiss on the cheek, and I melt. When I first met him, I was positive that his kindness was just an act, but now I'm not so sure. He might actually be a real gentleman. Crazy, right?

"Good morning. I was just appreciating the view."

His hands pull my hips against his body. "So was I."

We kiss for a few moments. He's an amazing kisser. When he kisses me, the whole world melts away.

"When are we heading to the expo?"

The expo. You're here for the expo.

I want to blow the full thing off and blow Preston instead. Spending all day with Preston in bed would be a dream, but I refuse to let my clit rule my brain.

"In a few hours. We can go to breakfast, or we can order room service. The restaurant downstairs overlooks the ocean also, but then again so does this room."

"We can go to dinner at a restaurant. I just want to eat out here if that's okay with you. Where's the menu?"

He goes inside and returns with the menu. I order island papaya and some Li Hing pineapple pancakes after I verify that they are vegan.

I excuse myself to hop in the shower. As the hot water cascades over my body, I marvel at this day. I still can't believe I'm in Hawai'i. Maybe after spending my entire life taking care of others, someone will finally take care of me.

I emerge from the shower. Preston is now dressed in a Hawaiian shirt and khaki shorts.

The waiter shows up. He sets up our spread on the little table outside. Preston pours me coffee once it has brewed in the French press.

"Sorry, I guess they don't have oat milk."

"It's okay. Coconut is fine."

I take a sip and am in heaven. I pour coconut syrup over my Li Hing pancakes, cut off a piece, and take a bite. My taste buds dance inside my mouth.

Preston, on the other hand, is devouring a lobster benedict. I try to bite my tongue and not go into a verbal tirade. I shouldn't impose my beliefs on others, but I can't help myself.

"How's the lobster? You know they scream when they are boiled alive. They're smart animals and feel pain."

Preston smirks. "Tasty little guys," he says after he shoves another piece of lobster in his mouth. "Look, Yessi. I may stop selling puppies, but no way in hell am I going to become vegan. I'll always eat meat. And lobsters."

I try not to lose my appetite. "You know you can fully subside on vegan food. In fact, several bodybuilders are vegan. I can show you how."

"Not gonna happen," he says as he takes another big bite of the lobster. I picture the lobster in my mind, his claws flailing in the air as he is slowly lowered into the boiling water to his death. I hear the cries he makes in my head. Tears well in my eyes.

I sometimes wish I didn't feel like this. Why do I care so much about animals' pain?

Preston puts his fork down. "You okay?"

"No. But don't stop eating on my accord. I mean, he died for your breakfast. Don't waste his life."

Preston rolls his eyes at me. "Seriously, stop. This is the natural way of life. We are top of the food chain. We are carnivores."

"Humans don't need meat to survive. I give fish to my cats because they need the taurine, but we don't need it."

"Didn't you tell me yesterday to buy a hamburger for Cuffs?"

"Yes, I did, because that poor dog was starving and it's dangerous to serve dogs or cats vegan food. I was trying to make him trust us, but we don't need meat, and we certainly don't need to eat animals that are killed in an inhumane way. I suppose you like *foie gras* also. And veal."

"Yup. Love them both. Look, I like you, Yessi, but I'm not going to ever change who I am for a woman. I won't live an inauthentic life. I do think that I could be wrong about selling puppies, but I'm going to eat meat. And lobster. And whatever the fuck I want. If that's a deal breaker for you, then let's end this now."

I sulk and turn away from him. If I had described my dream man, physically, it would be Preston, but philosophically, it most certainly would not be. I had pictured my perfect mate as a socially conscious man, a pacifist, an animal lover, an activist, and yes, a vegan. Bonus points if he loved hot yoga.

And, my ex had met all those requirements. He was nowhere near as hot as Preston is, though.

And my ex was a jerk. A complete and total asshat. He was mean and controlling. And a cheater. And he had been the one to call animal control on me after we broke up.

So, maybe, what I think I want isn't what I need. Perhaps I could be happy with a man like Preston.

I should stop being so judgy. I don't get mad at my pets when they eat meat. So why should I get mad at Preston?

I exhale and take a sip of my Kona coffee. "I don't want to end this now. For some reason despite myself, I like you."

"I like you, too."

I enjoy the rest of my breakfast and don't once fixate on the plump pink flesh of the lobster that Preston is eating.

CHAPTER FOURTEEN

PRESTON

After breakfast, we head down to the lobby and hail a taxi. Time to go to the expo.

I did my best to control my temper at breakfast, but I won't tolerate being nagged at for who I am. One of the things I like about Yessi is that being with her will allow me to open my eyes up to a different, more peaceful way of life. While I'm really leaning toward deciding to not sell puppies at Doggy Style, I will always eat meat. I want to enjoy my life. I want to indulge in the pleasures of the flesh and the joys of fine cuisine. I want to live my life to the fullest. Over in Iraq, I realized that, at any moment, my time could be up. My buddies died over there, gave their lives for our country, so I vowed to live every day like it is my last, and dammit, if I want a juicy steak and butter poached lobster, I'm going to have it.

Yessi didn't bring it up again. She's sitting next to me in the back of the taxi wearing a sexy sundress that I want to rip off of her. I snuck a peek of her pink lace panties when the trade winds blew up her dress outside. I can't wait to get this stupid expo over with, so I can take her back to the room and finally fuck her.

We finally arrive at the Hawaiian convention center. I pay and tip the driver, and we walk into the building. There are vendors everywhere. I'm overwhelmed by the site of leashes, collars, dog clothes, and, hell, even cat sweaters. Would cats even wear something like that?

I squeeze Yessi's hand. Coming here was so important to her. I want to make sure she gets everything she wants out of it. "Where do you want to go first?"

She thumbs a schedule that she picked up at a table by the door. "Well, it kicks off with the keynote on No-Kill USA by 2025. Then there's a talk about fundraising for rescues at ten, and, at noon, there is a talk on reimagining your dog adoption strategy, followed by a class on creating powerful content for showcasing your adoptable pets. I'm so excited!"

I'd rather stick a fork in my eyeball. "Sounds fascinating. Hey, why don't you go to the talks, and I'll walk around here and look at products. Then we can get out of here."

Her face drops. "I thought you wanted to go with me. I thought you wanted to learn."

No, I wanted to get laid. Ah fuck. This means the world to her. I have to make an effort. "I do. Hey, I'm sorry. I'm not a conference kind of guy. I wasn't any good at school, and I hate being at lectures—but I'll go with you."

"Thanks."

Kill me now. I follow Yessi like a love-sick puppy to the first lecture hall. The place is crowded with a bunch of women, most of them way older than Yessi. I stick out like a dick on a cake.

Yessi is introducing herself to people, but she noticeably doesn't introduce me. I guess hanging with a puppy store owner would hurt her street cred.

Finally, a lady with grey hair and a kind smile begins to speak. The lights dim, and I stare at the screen on the wall. Once the lecturer starts showing slides of all the homeless dogs in shelters and the abused dogs at breeders, I choke back tears. It's worse than watching that Sarah McLachlan's Angel video.

Fuck. Images flood my head. These poor dogs. Suffering. Killed in gas chambers. Abused. Bred and that tossed out like trash.

And I'm contributing to this problem. What the fuck is wrong with me?

There are so many great homeless pets who need homes. Like Gidget and Cuffs. These shelter dogs get killed every day because people would rather buy cute puppies like the ones I'm selling. But I can make a difference. I can showcase adoptable homeless pets. With Yessi's help, we can save thousands of dogs.

I don't need any more time. I make my final decision on the spot. I text Hugh.

> **Preston:** Cancel all puppy orders. We are only going to adopt out rescue pets.

Yessi is enthralled by the talk, scribbling notes and openly crying when she sees the pictures of the pets. I squeeze her thigh and show the text I sent to Hugh.

She smiles and kisses me in front of the entire room. "Thank you."

I kiss her back. In just a few days, she has already changed my life.

I'm not even doing this for her. I'm committed to saving as many dogs as I can. Maybe this is what I was meant to do all along.

I glance down at my phone.

> **Hugh:** Not a chance, asshole. I don't care how good her pussy is. It's my business too.

Fuck. He is a partner in this business. I quickly hide my phone. I don't want Yessi to see that message. I'll deal with Hugh later tonight.

The lecture ends, and Yessi and I walk out of the room.

And run straight into my parents.

Fuck.

A look of disgust registers on my father's face. I pause for a moment, not sure if I should reach out my hand to shake his or attempt a hug.

"Preston."

"Sir. I didn't think you would be here."

"Your mother wanted to come. I didn't know you would be here, or I wouldn't have attended."

Thanks, Dad.

My mom looks beautiful as always. She hugs me, and I hug her back. "So great to see you. Who is this lovely lady?"

"This is Yessi. She runs a dog rescue in Southern California."

My dad eyes Yessi hard, focusing on her tattoos. "Is she your girlfriend or just another one of the girls you use and discard?"

Damn, why does he have to be such a dick? I grab Yessi's hand and notice that her cheeks are red. We have definitely not had the defining the relationship talk. "It's new and we are dating. I'm crazy about her. You will really like her too. She's smart and compassionate and isn't afraid to stand up to me."

Yessi smiles and squeezes my hand. "Nice to meet you, Mr. Evans. You must be very proud of Preston. His new store is beautiful and will definitely be a success, especially since he just made the decision to no longer sell puppies and only showcase rescue dogs in his store. He will be saving so many lives."

My mom brightens up. "Oh Preston, that's wonderful."

My father, however, remains stoic. "Nice to meet you, Yessi. You seem like a smart young lady but let me give you a tip about my son—don't believe a word he says. He's probably using you for publicity like he uses everyone."

I clench my fist. I need to get out of here before I say or do something I will regret. "Bye, Mom."

I walk out of the expo and head to the beach.

CHAPTER FIFTEEN

YESSI

I force myself to say goodbye to Preston's parents. "Nice to meet you, Mr. and Mrs. Evans." Before they can respond, I dash out of the building and race after Preston.

Wow. For years I fantasized about what it would be like to have parents who actually took the time to raise me. I pitied myself for growing up in a foster home, for aging out at eighteen and having no one to call my family.

But seeing the way Preston's father just spoke to him makes me wonder if I'm better off. I knew my family didn't care about me. I didn't need to earn their approval. I live my life just for myself.

Preston is at the corner of the road, smoking a cigarette with some guy. Damn, I didn't know that Preston smoked.

He glances up at me as the other guy walks away. "Just leave me alone. Go back to your conference. I'll meet you back at the hotel."

"I just want to be with you."

He takes a drag on his cigarette. "Yeah, what? I smoke. You were right about me. I'm an asshole. Clearly, my dad thinks so, too. I'm never going to be good enough for him, or you, so let's just forget this ever happened."

I reach out and take his hand. "Obviously there is obviously more going on with you and your dad than just the sex tape, and I'm happy to listen to you, but I'm not going anywhere. Especially since we came here together. I like you. You aren't perfect, but neither am I."

"You seem perfect to me. You are beautiful, kind, and spend your entire life saving homeless pets. You're practically Mother Theresa."

I laugh. "No, I'm a mess. I'm way too judgmental and closed off."

He flicks the cigarette on the ground and stomps on it.

I don't want to sound like a nag, but I'm curious because I

haven't seen him smoke around me or smelled cigarettes on his breath or clothes. Maybe he would sneak out for a smoke when I wasn't looking. "I haven't seen you smoke. Is it just a casual thing or are you a pack a day kind of guy?"

"I don't really smoke anymore. I just bummed a cigarette off that guy. It's a nasty habit I picked up in Iraq."

I nod my head. "I get it. War seems like a good excuse to smoke. I used to smoke, too."

"Really? When?"

"When I was in my group home. I grew up in foster care. It was my I-Hate-Everyone stage." I'm actually still in that stage, but he doesn't need the details.

His angry scowl drops off his face, replaced by a look of compassion toward me. "Sorry, I just acted like a bitch, whining about my daddy problems. I didn't know you grew up in foster care."

"Yeah, I don't tell people that. Like, ever. I don't like to talk about it."

He bites his lip and then digs into his pocket and stuffs a stick of gum in his mouth.

"I don't blame you. I don't like to talk much either."

"Then let's not talk much together. Let's go. We can go anywhere you want. Back to the hotel. Get something to eat. I don't need to go back to the expo today." It's all weekend. We can come back tomorrow. I'm just grateful to be here.

"Can we go to the beach?"

"I'd like that."

We walk down the road toward the beach. We finally make it to the sand and take off our shoes. The warmth of the sand envelops my feet, and the fragrant ocean breeze relaxes me immediately.

Preston takes my hand. It's a beautiful moment, one that strikes me as sweet and intimate. "How did you quit? Smoking, I mean?"

"Oh, I had to stop when I became vegan. The tobacco companies test on animals, so I just gave it up."

He shakes his head. "It was just that easy for you? One day, 'I'm vegan—don't need this addictive nicotine.' You didn't get withdrawals? Every time I get stressed out, I crave a cigarette."

"I never said it was easy. Being vegan isn't easy either. But nothing worth doing in life is."

His hand reaches around my neck, and he pulls me in to kiss him. I don't even mind the hint of tobacco on his breath, which is now mixed in with the aftertaste of his minty gum. He cups my head in his hands and just looks at me. "Why are you so driven, so selfless?"

"I don't know. I just believe that saving animals is my purpose in life. My cause. Animals were the only living beings who cared for me when I was in foster care. So, I devoted my life to helping them. It's simple really. I have no one else. Well Eden and Avril, but that's about it." The second those words leave my mouth I realize how pathetic they sound, but I trust that Preston won't judge me for them.

"You have me."

Swoon. We kiss in the sand, and the world melts away between us. I have no idea why Preston moves me so much, not just physically, but emotionally. All I know, is kissing him on the beach in Hawai'i is the happiest moment of my life.

Preston whispers in my ear. "Let's go back to the room."

CHAPTER SIXTEEN

PRESTON

I hail a cab, and we get in the back seat and start kissing. Her skin smells like coconut lotion and papaya. "Why do you taste so sweet?"

"Vegans taste better."

Ha. I'm a few days into our relationship and already addicted to her scent, her taste, her touch. Even crazier is that I've already agreed to throw away my whole business model to please her, though I've now been convinced by that it is the right thing to do.

What would it be like to be in a long-term relationship with Yessi? Would I become a better man? Or would I never be good enough for a woman like her?

The taxi arrives at the hotel. I pay the guy and, just like yesterday, we race to the room. I vow to actually explore this beautiful resort, but not now. Later.

After I fuck Yessi.

Our kissing recommences in the elevator, but this time, I won't be satisfied just to taste her.

When we reach the room, I open the door, turn her around, and throw her over the back of the sofa. I hike up her sundress, and my hands grip her incredible ass as I kiss her neck.

"Oh, Pres."

"Don't go anywhere." I slap her ass and dash to the bathroom to get a condom. When I return, she's still bent over the sofa, waiting for me. "Come here, baby."

She walks over to me, and I scoop her up and carry her to the coffee table. I'm dying to fuck her, but I'm a patient man. I want her wet and ready for me.

I remove her pink lace panties and spread her legs wide. I kneel before her and lick her pussy, eating her, devouring her, lapping up her sweetness. Her breath starts to sputter. I slide my finger inside of her, and she's so incredibly tight. She moans, and her cheeks flush.

"Pres! Just fuck me."

Yes, ma'am.

"On all fours," I bark.

She obediently hops off the table and climbs on the sofa. Her sundress is still on, and I find it so incredibly hot that her bare-naked ass is sticking up in the air while the thin material covers the rest of her banging body.

I can't wait any longer to fuck her.

I roll the condom on over my cock and climb behind her on the sofa. I rub her pussy again, and she's so wet, so ready for me.

I tap the head of my cock against her pussy and slowly slide it in as she gasps. "You okay, baby? You like my cock?"

"Yes, I love it."

Bingo. She pushes her ass back, pressing it against my crotch. And I'm lost inside her. She's so hot. The view of her plump ass is almost too much to handle. Her pussy clamps around my cock and I'm already in pure ecstasy. The harder I fuck her, the harder she fucks me back, moving her ass back and forth, meeting every thrust. My hand rubs her clit, and her breath speeds up.

"That's it, baby. Come all over my cock."

She whimpers. I need to see her face, I need to connect with her, I want more than just sex from her. I want passion. I want intimacy. I want acceptance.

I want love.

I pull out of her and sit back down on the sofa and turn her to face me. "Let me see you, beautiful. Come here."

I'm done with her dress now. I pull it off over her head, and her long black hair cascades over her nipples. I take a mental picture of this moment. This is the first time we will ever have sex.

And, hopefully, Yessi will be the last girl I will ever have sex with.

She climbs on my lap and this time she's in control of the motion. She lowers herself down on my cock, slowly, so slowly.

Finally, we are fully connected. Man and woman. Mind, body, and soul.

She rocks and rolls on me, the most beautiful sight I have ever seen. Her rhythm quickens, and I know she's close.

I nuzzle my head on her chest and lower my mouth to her

nipple. I take the pierced one into my mouth, and she moans. She tosses her head back, and I clamp my hands down on her hips, guiding her movement, bringing her closer to the edge and then forcing her back down again.

"Make me feel good," she screams.

I grind her down on my cock again and suck on her tits until she lets out a long cry. Her pussy clamps and releases around my cock and I allow myself to let go, exploding in a moment of ecstasy.

I stop for a moment and look into her eyes. "I'm crazy about you."

"Me, too. That was . . . that was amazing."

I kiss her forehead. She climbs off my lap and runs off to the bathroom. I head to the other bathroom to clean up.

I start making plans for the rest of the day. What would she enjoy? I want to spoil her. Well, a luau is out. No pig roasted in the ground for Yessi. A romantic dinner on the beach? A moonlit swim in the ocean? A live concert at a local bar?

I reach my phone to look up who's playing near our hotel, and I see three missed calls.

I check the voicemail.

"Preston Evans, this is Deb Ramos at the HB animal shelter. A dog microchipped to you was just dumped in the night drop. Do you want to surrender her to the shelter?"

CHAPTER SEVENTEEN

YESSI

Preston's face goes white when he listens to his phone. I wonder if his dad texted him.

Before I ask, I take a moment to marvel at how incredible our sex was. It was completely amazing. I'm blown away. I came so fucking hard. His cock is so huge, and, more importantly, he knows how to use it.

All that virile man prowess aside, there were other moments that were even more special. The way he looked at me while we had sex. The way he connected with me on a deeper level. It felt emotional, intimate. He was completely tuned into my wants, my needs. I never once felt that he was just trying to get himself off.

It's as if he completely cares for me.

Don't be silly, Yessi. You have known this dude for exactly four days. You are so pathetic. He's going to be just like every other person you have met in your life. He's going to use and abandon you.

I shake these self-deprecating thoughts off. No. Maybe it will be different this time. Maybe after all these years of being discarded by everyone I have ever cared about, I've finally met someone who will be there for me.

Preston paces and starts frantically dialing a number.

"You okay?"

He lets out a long exhale. "No. Don't freak out, but I just got a call from the shelter. They have Gidget."

A heaviness settles deep in my stomach. No, this can't be happening.

"What? Are you sure? How did she get there? She's supposed to be in your shop. How did they get your number?"

"I microchipped her before the day after I got her. She was left in the night drop."

Adrenalin rushes through my body, and I take every inch of self-control I have not to fly into a rage. "The fucking night drop? Who dumped her in the night drop?"

"I don't know. I'm going to find out." He tries to put his arms on my shoulders, but I push him off. "It's going to be okay, Yessi. Don't worry. I'll just call Hugh—"

I point my finger at him. "Don't you dare fucking call Hugh. I saw the way he looked at her. I heard what he said about her. He is the one who probably dumped her."

I run over and grab my own phone from my purse. "I'll call Eden now to send in a pull and have Avril pick her up. Which shelter?"

"I don't think Hugh would dump her. Let me just call—"

"I said I'll handle it. I swear to god, Evans, if anything happens to Gidget, I'm going to hold you personally accountable. Which fucking shelter?"

He tells me, and I call Eden.

Eden answers on the first ring. "Hey! How's Hawai'i?"

"Beautiful, but I'm coming home. I need you to do me a favor. Can you call in a pull for Gidget?"

"Gidget? The dog Preston was fostering?"

"Yup. She was dumped in the night drop. I'll figure it out. I mean, Preston's with me now, so I'm going to try not to blame him, but, clearly, our dogs aren't safe at his store.

Can you and Avril get her and then go to the store to check on them? Like now?"

"Yup. I'll call her. Are you okay?"

"Yeah. I was having a great time, but now I'm stressed. I'm going to take the next flight home. Oh, and I found a pit bull here."

"Of course, you did. All right. Text me your flight info. I'll text you back when we get Gidget and the rest of the dogs."

"Thanks, babe. Love you," I say because I do. I love Eden and Avril. I trust them, and they are the only people who love me back.

I hang up the phone and go into the bedroom to pack. I don't have enough money for a last-minute ticket home, but, hopefully, the change fee won't be too expensive.

Preston appears in the doorway. "Hey, can we talk?"

I exhale.

Breathe, Yessi, breathe. Preston did not dump Gidget in the night drop. He was with you the entire time. Fucking you, as a matter of fact. You owe it to him to hear his side of the story.

"Fine, talk. Have you gotten a hold of Hugh? What's his pathetic ass excuse? Are all our other dogs dumped in night drops?"

"I can't get a hold of Hugh, but when I do, I'll figure out what the fuck happened. If he did anything shady, I'll personally fuck him up. I called the kennel tech at the store. She said all the other dogs, including your rescue dogs, are fine. She said that Hugh took Gidget home with him last night and he didn't come into work today, so she assumed that Gidget was with him. Maybe she got loose, and someone else dumped her?"

I shake my head in disbelief. "Are you that gullible? Clearly, Hugh dumped her. It's too much of a coincidence that she is the only dog he took home and she just happened to end up in the night drop. Good news is we can solve this riddle. I know Deb from the shelter. All she has to do is look at the video footage on the camera, and we can see who dumped her. If it's Hugh, I'll beat his ass myself."

I grab the shirt I wore yesterday and toss into my suitcase. I crumple up the fabric as my heart constricts in my chest.

I picture sweet Gidget, only a few days after being dumped by the only family she has ever known, being thrown away like yesterday's trash. Shivering in that cold, dank cage, her eyes blinking back tears, with all the rest of the dumped pets. Only cowards drop their pets in the night drop. What does it say about Preston that this motherfucker is his best friend?

Thank God Preston had chipped her, or she would've most certainly died. I kick myself for not chipping her myself. For going on this trip. For trusting Preston.

And I can't help it. I begin to sob.

Preston kneels by my side and holds me in his arms. "Hey, babe. Look at me."

I look away because I have the maturity of a five-year-old. I'm emotionally stunted. Five. Five was the age that my parents left me. Five was the last time in my life that I had a home. That I had a family.

And I was never adopted. Because everyone wants a cute baby. Nobody wants to adopt the quiet girl who does nothing all day but sketch in her notepad and play with stray pets.

Kind of like how no one wants to adopt the old dog with a grey mug who just wants to sleep all day.

Ugh, I'm a mess.

"Look at me."

I look up at him, my eyes all blotchy, with mascara running down my face.

"I'm taking complete responsibility for this. I don't know what happened, but I'm going to get to the bottom of this. If Hugh dumped Gidget in the night drop—and I just can't believe it until I have proof—then I will destroy him. I mean it. Gidget is a great dog. I care about her life. She doesn't deserve that shit. Whatever you need me to do, I'm on it. Please don't shut me out. How can I help?"

I surrender. I need his help. For once, I can't do this on my own. "Can we just get out of here? Can we fly back tonight?"

"Yup. I'll call now. Yessi, I'm so sorry. What about Cuffs?"

Fuck, I need to take care of Cuffs. "I'll call the vet now. I doubt he's ready to fly and even if he were, he would need shots and a health certificate. Do you have any friends who can take him until we can arrange for transport?"

His face turns stern. "My father. He loves dogs, but he hates me. Don't worry. I'll figure it out. Worst case scenario, he can stay at the vet or at boarding."

I exhale. I'm not going to write Preston off yet. "Thanks. It means a lot to me."

"Not as much as you mean to me. I'm going to fix this, Yessi. Just give me a chance to fix things."

I nod. I hear Preston call the airline.

After years of taking care of everyone else, it's nice to have someone take care of me.

CHAPTER EIGHTEEN

PRESTON

The plane touches down in L.A. I quickly turn on my phone to see if there is an update from Hugh, but there is nothing.

Dude is fucking ghosting me.

What the fuck?

Did he purposely dump Gidget in the night drop? I can't believe it.

But if he didn't, he would be returning my calls.

I look over and see Yessi frantically typing on her phone.

"Good news. Avril picked up Gidget. And the shelter won't charge you any fees because you didn't dump her. I'm still pissed as hell, but at least she's safe."

Thank God.

"But, there's more. Look at this."

She shows her phone to me, and my stomach wrenches when I see the picture. There, clear as a Honolulu sunrise, is a photo of Hugh placing Gidget in a cage at the night drop.

I'm going to fucking kill him. I'm not going to lie and make excuses for him anymore.

"Yeah, that's him. I'm speechless. I knew he was kind of a dick, but I can't believe he would just toss her away like that in the middle of the night.

"Well, he did buddy. And I will work with you in the pet store, even though you have breeder puppies there, because you agreed to make your store an adoption center. But I will not set foot in that store, except, of course, to get our dogs, if Hugh still works there. There is no logical explanation for what he did. No hope for redemption. Dude is a piece of shit. What is he going to say? That he accidentally dumped her at the night drop?"

She has a point. Man, I don't want to deal with this shit. Hugh ruined my trip to Hawai'i, endangered Gidget, and put a strain on my relationship with Yessi. How could I be so wrong about this guy? Did I just blindly trust him because I grew up with him? What is his motivation for doing that? Sabotaging me? Does he hate me? If so, why?

I'm going to find out

I grab our bags, and we leave the airplane and head to baggage claim. I wanted to hire a limo, but Eden insisted on picking us up.

The last people I want to hang out with right now are Yessi's rescue mafia. I already know I royally fucked up. I don't need the additional stress of being interrogated for the entire ride home.

Eden pulls up in an old VW van with the Pugs N Roses logo emblazoned on the side. I choke on the smoggy L.A. air and miss Hawai'i immediately. Avril jumps out of the car.

"Hey girl!"

She embraces Yessi. I'm happy that Yessi has such close friends, especially after she told me about growing up in foster care. I still have so many questions to ask her, but I'm not sure if she wants to talk about it.

"Evans," Avril says curtly.

"Avril." I don't know her last name. I just know that she's really suspicious of me, but I hope I can win her over.

I climb into the van and smile when I see Gidget. She greets me with a lick. "Hey, girl." She wiggles her little butt, and I rub her belly. A lump grows in my throat. Why did Hugh drop her at the shelter? She could've been killed. I would've never forgiven myself.

Seeing Gidget's sweet face wrecks me with guilt.

I get it.

I get why Yessi, Eden, and Avril, devote their lives to saving dogs.

"Hey, Preston. Did you have a nice trip?" Eden seems sincere and less judgy than Avril.

"Hawai'i is always great. Too bad it was cut short. But, at least, we saved a dog." I bring up finding Cuffs to deflect off the Gidget situation.

"Oh, the 'pibble?' Yeah, they are always hard to adopt. So, you're going to adopt him, too, right?" Avril starts in with the guilt trip.

"We will see." Man, I'm going to end up going from zero dogs to two. And Yessi has six. If we ever move in together, we will have eight dogs. Is that even legal?

Gidget curls into my lap, and I take Yessi's hand. "Can we go straight to my store? I need to find Hugh."

Eden looks over to me. "Well, we went by this morning. Our dogs are all fine. Hugh was not there."

What the fuck? He lives above the store. How could he not be there?

"Could you please just take me there? I'll check around his place. He lives above the shop."

"Sure," she says.

After a few hours in horrendous L.A. traffic, we finally arrive at the store. We all pile out of the van and go inside. First, we check on the dogs, who are all in great condition.

I see Wanda, the kennel attendant. "Hey, Wanda. Thanks for holding this place down for me. Have you seen Hugh?"

She shakes her head. "No. Not for a couple of days. He took off with Gidget and a duffel bag. Said he was staying at your place. I didn't ask no questions him. He hasn't been back since."

My place? I told him he couldn't stay at my home if he wouldn't watch Gidget. What a jerk.

But he does have a spare key to my condo.

As do I to his place.

I dash upstairs and enter his apartment. I see a half-eaten bowl of cereal on the kitchen table, dirty laundry on the floor, and an overflowing garbage can in the kitchen. It's a pigsty, but nothing out of the ordinary. Dude is a slob—it always looks like that.

But there is no sign of Hugh.

I text him again.

> **Preston:** Dude. Where the fuck are you? We open in two days. We need to talk.

I stare at my phone but get no reply.

I run downstairs. Yessi greets me, holding a fluffy poodle.

"Where is he? Let me at him," she says, with a smirk on her face.

"No clue, but I'm screwed. I'm supposed to open this place in a few days. I need him."

She takes my hands. "No, you don't. You got us."

CHAPTER NINETEEN

YESSI

few days later, we arrive at the crack of dawn at Doggy Style.

It's opening day.

A mixture of hopefulness and despair stirs inside me. I pray that we will adopt out a ton of dogs today. Obviously, finding them homes will be the greatest reward, but I also want to prove to Preston that customers will adopt these rescue dogs and he doesn't need to sell puppies. I know he has agreed to only feature rescue dogs, but I want to show him that he can have a successful business without using breeder dogs. Of course, we still have the purebred puppies in the store until they are all sold. And I've come to peace with that, though I'm requiring Preston to follow standard adoption protocol on all dogs. All of the dogs have been fixed, every owner will be required to submit to a home check and complete an adoption application and contract.

As for my personal growth, I've vowed the other day to try to be less judgmental. I can't hate on people who don't know any better, so I need to educate them. I will be calm, friendly, and sweet. Preston is the perfect example. He didn't know about the horrors of homeless pets, and then he learned. Now, he has changed his mind and will end up saving thousands of pets.

Preston paces around the store, his hand clutching his phone.

I walk over to him and give him a kiss. "You okay?"

"Yeah. I just need this to do well. I was so confident, but I can't believe Hugh bailed. I just have a bad feeling, you know? Like he's going to do something to fuck the opening up."

Hugh has vanished. No one has seen him since he left the store that day with Gidget. He also hasn't been on any social media. Preston has called him a bunch of times, reached out to Hugh's parents, even considered filing a police report, but I told him to hold off. Clearly, Hugh has some anger and resentment toward Preston. I believe Hugh left on his own accord to prove a point to Preston that the store would fail with the rescue dogs. Of course, I could be wrong, and I don't know the dude at all, but if something happened to him, he wouldn't have dropped Gidget off in the night drop.

"Well, he better not, but we will be okay no matter what. Avril and Eden are here to help. I've promoted it on all our rescue groups. It will be great. People will be so glad that you are going to be saving so many lives. And this store is beautiful. It's owner's not bad either."

He pulls me to him, and we kiss. We've been fucking like rabbits since we arrived back in California. I've never had sexual chemistry with anyone like I have with Preston. Everything about him is perfection.

Even so, our emotional intimacy hasn't caught up to our physical intimacy. I still don't know the details about his dad, and I still haven't told him about my past. But I'm not worried about that. We started fast, so it's fine to take our time opening up to each other.

Avril stands in front of us. We break our kiss and stare at her.

"Come on. Time to open."

We all go outside. The mayor of Huntington Beach is waiting for Preston, and he hands Preston huge scissors to cut off the bow.

Preston whispers in my ear, "I'd rather have your handcuffs."

I playfully smack him. "Where are those things anyway?"

"You'll see them when the time is right."

I roll my eyes.

Preston greets the crowd. "Thank you for coming out today. Initially, I started this store to just make a profit off of dogs. I know, it sounds horrible, and it was. But then I met this gorgeous woman, Yesenia Cordova, and she educated me about shelter dogs. I honestly never knew much about homeless pets. She has changed my life, and I'm just glad that she opened my eyes up to their plights. I'm so thankful for taking this journey with her, and even more happy that she is now my girlfriend. So, everyone, welcome to Doggy Style!"

Oh my God.

Tears well in my eyes. I didn't expect him to say anything like that. Here I am, crying on camera like a blubbering fool. No one has ever done anything like that for me. Or even publicly acknowledged me as part of their life. I've always been the foster kid, the side chick, the girl to be hidden.

I wrap my arms around Preston and kiss him again. Cameras flash in our face. And I'm no longer a secret.

CHAPTER TWENTY

PRESTON

"That will be one thousand five hundred dollars," I say to the family who is about to purchase a purebred British bulldog.

Yessi scowls at them. She had tried in vain to convince them to adopt a dachshund mix, but they wouldn't budge.

I get it. For years, all I wanted was a bulldog, the mascot of my beloved Marine Corps. I wanted to name him Grady, after my buddy who was awarded the Medal of Honor. Half of Grady's face was blown off, but he was lucky enough to live. He found himself a beautiful wife, Isa, and is now speaking on college campuses. I fucking love that guy. If it weren't for him, I'd be dead.

The family beams at their new puppy. "Oh, we can't wait to breed her!"

Oh fuck. I don't even need to look at Yessi. I know she's going to go off.

"Well, too bad for that, because all of our dogs are fixed, including the puppies."

The man's eyes bug. "Fixed? You fixed all the puppies?"

"Yes. She is actually four months old. She was fixed last week. Invisible stitches so they don't need to be removed. But our adoption policy requires all dogs to be fixed before placement. When would you like to set up your home check?"

His eyes glaze over. "Home check? Lady, we are about to spend one thousand five hundred dollars on this puppy. And you fixed her, so we can't make our money back. Now you want to come to our home too? What else do you want? Our first-born child?"

I want to laugh but decide to hold my tongue.

Yessi calmly continues, "We understand how much money you are about to pay. You are very lucky to get this puppy, as she will be one of the last purebred bulldog puppies we will get. We are turning the store into a shelter only adoption center. Home checks are required. We aren't trying to judge the way you live, but we need to make sure that you have a secure fence and gate around your pool. You don't have to buy this dog. It's your choice."

The man's little girl bites her lower lip. "Please, daddy? You said we could get a puppy."

He kneels to her. "But Princess, we wanted to get her, so you could witness the miracle of birth."

I reach my hand out to stop Yessi before she launches into a verbal tirade.

"The miracle of birth? What a joke. Want to see the results of that miracle? Go visit the local animal shelter and see all the homeless dogs there who will be slaughtered because of people like you who want to breed puppies."

Yessi picks up the bulldog and takes it back to her cage.

"Hey, that's my dog. Bring her back."

"Sorry, sir, you are not approved to adopt her," Yessi yells.

Oh fuck. "Excuse me. I'm sorry about her. She's a bit on edge. Please wait here. I'll be right back."

I race over to Yessi. "Babe, come on. You can't just deny them because they want to breed her."

"Yes, I can. And I just did. This is my rescue, and now all the dogs' adoptions are done through the rescue, including your puppies. Once you agreed to use our adoption contract, Pugs N Roses is liable for all these dogs. I don't think they are the right fit for this puppy."

Breathe, Preston, breathe. "You haven't done the home check yet. You could at least check them out and see."

"See what? Where they planned to breed her?"

I'm crazy about this woman but she drives me insane. "Yessi, dammit. They want to adopt. Give them a chance."

She grabs their app. "Did you see this? They want to crate her. Who would crate a puppy! It's not good to crate bull-dogs or pugs because of their snub noses. I bet they will lock her up in a crate all day." She pets the bulldog. "Poor baby doesn't want to be in a crate, do you? You're a good girl. Yes, you are."

"You're unbelievable."

Yessi pouts like a child, but I have a hard time saying no to her. "No, I'm not. I just want the perfect home for her.

We can find an amazing family with bully experience. Maybe someone who has senior bulldogs and will never ever buy one. I can list her. Don't make me give her to them."

I turn around and see the family walking out of the door.

Great.

"See, they didn't want her anyway,"

"Yessi! Are you serious right now? I needed that sale. We won't be making much on your rescue dogs. I need a way to pay the rent. Especially because I can't get a hold of fucking Hugh."

Hugh. Where the fuck was Hugh? I was sure he would resurface by now.

"You don't need Hugh. You are so much better than that guy. Don't sink to his level. You will have to switch your business model. We can do yappy hours, puglates, doga? Maybe your ex can teach a class here."

"Doubtful. She flaked on the opening. Look, I'm happy you and your friends are working with me, especially since Hugh no-showed, but you can't drive customers away. They will kill us in Yelp reviews."

The bulldog moans when Yessi rubs his ear. "Fine. I'm

sorry. I'll try to relax. Being around all these breeder puppies is hard for me. I'll make it up to you."

Now we're talking. I lower my voice. "What did you have in mind?"

"I'll show you later tonight."

CHAPTER TWENTY-ONE

YESSI

After another long day at the shop, we are finally closed. We secure all the dogs in their kennels for the night, say goodbye to Wanda, Avril, and Eden, leash up Gidget, and leave the store.

In the week since the store has been opened, I have spent every night with Preston, but it wasn't just because I wanted to spend time with him. My landlord raised my rent. All of my own dogs are staying with Avril, and all of my foster dogs are staying at the store. Next week, I'll look for a new place, but until then, I'm happy that Preston has been so gracious and let me stay with him.

And we've had fun. We like the same type of movies (horror), music (heavy metal), and books (true crime).

But one thing we haven't done is talk.

I mean really talk.

I want to break his shell. I want to understand what is going on with his father.

And I want to open up to him about my own past. If he's going to run away, I need to know now before I get even more attached to him.

Preston takes my hand. "Let's go to dinner. Have you been to Sharkeez? They are dog-friendly so we can bring Gidget."

"I love Sharkeez. They did a fundraiser once for Pugs N Roses."

"Cool. Let's walk."

We leave the store and walk hand in hand to Sharkeez. The sun begins to set, and the cool ocean breeze blows the days' worries away. I know I came off pretty harshly to that family that wanted to adopt Lola, the bully, but I don't care. I hope Preston doesn't resent me. I'll find her a good home.

The hostess seats us at a table. After we ask for some chips and guacamole, I order a hand-muddled strawberry margarita with Don Julio Blanco tequila and vegan enchiladas, and Preston orders a Corona and steak fajitas.

After a few sips of my margarita, my nerves relax. "Hey, sorry about earlier. That family just rubbed me the wrong way."

"It's okay. I didn't like them either. Just try to be a bit more patient when you explain to people about rescue dogs."

I try not to get annoyed by what he just said, but it's hard. I suppose he's right. I should be more positive and upbeat. Like Avril. Like Eden. I shake off my frustration.

The waitress brings us our chips and guacamole. I study Preston and notice him eyeing everyone in the restaurant. Not rude or like checking out other women, but just casing them, like he's either about to hold up this place, or arrest someone.

I exhale. Time to go deep. "So, what happened to you over in Iraq?"

His turn to exhale. He knocks back his beer. "We were clearing buildings. Some insurgent threw a hand grenade into the building. My buddy, Grady, jumped on it and saved our lives, though one of our buddies got blown to pieces. Grady's face was blown up, too." He speaks as if he is reciting a report, detached entirely, almost robotic.

I get it. I sometimes need to separate myself from emotion to hide my pain.

Wow. That's intense. I reach my hand to touch his. He doesn't pull his back. "I'm sorry, Preston. I had no idea."

"It's fine, I'm fine."

But he doesn't sound fine. I should move on, but I don't. "I don't get it. You're a war hero. Why does your dad hate you so much? Just because of the tape?"

His eyes glaze over. "Well, that put the nail in the coffin. He really believes I leaked that video. I didn't. He doesn't believe that a woman would leak it. Kira denied it to his face, as she did to mine, but he believes her and not me. But I promise you, Yessi, I didn't leak it. I don't know what to believe."

I need to let it go but I can't. "But that's it? He hates you so much because of that? There has to be more."

"I mean, of course, there's more. I was a punk ass kid before I joined the Corps. The Marines made me the man I am today. Dad had wanted me to move back home when I got out and work in his business. He runs a restaurant on the North Shore. But I wanted to make my own way, live in California. So, he thinks I sold out and ruined his name for the fame. I didn't, but he won't listen to me, so that's that."

"That's never that. I mean if I had a family, I would do anything to repair the relationship."

His shoulders drop, and he stares intensely into my eyes. I can see him soften. "Sorry, I sound like a selfish asshole. At least I have a family. Your turn, babe. Tell me about your past."

Well, I asked for it. No turning back now. "Not much to tell. My mom was a drug addict. I was lucky that she didn't use when she was pregnant with me, but after my dad left, she became a hooker and addicted to smack. Her family had disowned her. CPS took me in when I was five. They couldn't locate any of her family, or so they said. I think they did find her family, and they just didn't want me. Anyway, it took a while to go through the courts and terminate her rights, so I wasn't up for adoption until I was twelve. No one wanted to adopt a twelve-year-old. I even did one of those Wednesday's Child segments on television where they try to guilt people into adopting. For my day out, they took me to an animal shelter, and I started volunteering there but didn't get into rescuing until later. Back then, I would just read to the stray cats and dogs. So, after no one adopted me, I just aged out of the foster system. Met some guy, Juan. I always liked to draw, so he taught me how to tattoo. And that's that."

Preston blinks rapidly at me like my story is unbearably worse than his being blown up at war, which it's not. "Babe, I'm sorry. You are so strong and tough. I can't even imagine growing up like that."

"I'm fine. It's better in some ways. I have no one to disappoint. No one to tell me what to do." No one to love.

"Hey, stop. It's not better. Stop trying to make it seem like you are above love and pain. Being sad about it is okay. It's okay to dream of having a family. It's okay to want love."

Ah fuck. I do not want to cry. Not at all. The waitress brings our meals, and I eat in silence. I don't want to do this. I don't want to be vulnerable in front of Preston.

After dinner, we walk on the beach with Gidget.

Preston kisses me under the moonlight.

"Yessi, I know we haven't known each other long, but I think I love you."

My heart jumps through my chest. Loves me? It's so soon. Does he really mean it?

But I know he does. Because I feel it too.

"I love you too."

CHAPTER TWENTY-TWO

PRESTON

I awake in the morning to a sweet kiss, but I quickly realize that the giver of the affection is Gidget, not Yessi, who is still sound asleep, her long dark hair tousled on the pillow. She's so naturally gorgeous without a lick of makeup. I'm thankful that she's my woman. Though we are very different people and have different beliefs, we complement each other is so many ways.

I roll out of bed, pull on my pajama bottoms, grab my phone, and leash Gidget up. She stretches into a perfect downward dog and then reverses direction to an upward dog. I adore her, too. She's seriously the sweetest dog. I can't believe her owner, and Hugh, dumped her.

I take the elevator down to the grass area and let Gidget use the bathroom.

Time to reconnect with the digital world. I pick up my phone and see that it's blowing up with messages.

Damn, dawg, she's hot.

You're the man.

Dirty devil dog—can't believe you did another sex tape.

Wait—what the fuck?

My heart races in my chest. This can't be happening to me again.

I click on my SnapChat and see a bunch of messages.

And there it is—for the world to see.

A clip of me doing Yessi doggy style, in my apartment, the other week.

Rage boils through me. Did she leak this? I sure as hell didn't. Why the hell would she betray me? Did she use me to get publicity for her rescue? How did she film this? Is there a camera in my home?

Breathe, Preston. Breathe. Don't freak out. Calm under pressure. Think rationally and don't jump to conclusions.

No. No. No. It couldn't have been Yessi. That would make no sense. I don't believe that she would sell me out like that. Kira it made sense because she wanted to live in the limelight. But Yessi doesn't care about fame at all. She's happy taking moonlit strolls on the beach with me. We are already planning a trip back to Hawai'i to finish our vacation and get Cuffs, who has finally recovered from all of his illnesses. Poor guy had giardia, worms, mange, and a ton of other issues I can't even pronounce. The vet says he's the sweetest dog, and I'm just grateful that we saved him.

But Yessi wouldn't do this. And I didn't do this.

Then it hits me.

Hugh.

Oh my God! Hugh!

How could I have been such an idiot? He has a key to my place. Wanda told me that he said he was heading to my place when she saw last him. And I always let him stay at my place in the past when I was with Kira.

Kira.

Fuck. I blamed Kira for the tape. Wouldn't listen to her when she denied leaking it. I'm such an asshole. That tape ruined our relationship. I won't let that happen with Yessi.

Gidget finishes her business. My hand shakes as I hold her leash.

I race upstairs with Gidget in tow. Yessi is now in the kitchen brewing coffee. The aroma of the freshly ground beans mixed with the salty sea air fills my condo, but I feel anything but relaxed. I drop the leash and stand next to my bed, my eyes scanning like when I was a sniper.

"Pres, what are you doing? You look like you've seen a ghost."

I don't even answer her because I finally see it. A small red light, pointing at my skull like I'm a target.

That mother fucker. How did I never notice this? Some Marine I am—I'm supposed to be always aware of my surroundings. And not only could I not protect myself from this violation of privacy, but also, I can't protect my women.

I jump up on the bed and swap the camera down.

"Preston, what the fuck. Oh my God? Is that a camera?"

"Yup."

I peer into the camera. "Hey, Hugh, you motherfucker. I'm going to fucking destroy you. Stop being such a pussy and show your face."

I turn my attention to Yessi. Sweet Yessi. She's not even looking at her phone right now. Unlike me, she isn't glued to it twenty-four seven. She has a full life that doesn't involve technology. She spends her days reading, sketching, playing with her dogs, doing yoga, just being present. She has introduced such a level of calm into my life.

And she has no idea that our intimate moments have just been broadcast to the world.

"Babe, I need to talk to you."

Her eyes get big. "You're freaking me out, Pres. What's going on?"

I take a deep breath. I need her to believe me.

"I just saw that there was a tape of us leaked online."

She blinks rapidly. "A tape? What kind of tape?"

"A tape of us having sex. I swear to God I didn't know there was a camera up there. Hugh must've set it up. He has a key to my place. I bet he leaked the one with Kira also."

I study her face, expecting her to explode on me. But she doesn't yell. She doesn't accuse me.

Her shoulders drop, and she exhales. "I believe you. Hugh's a piece of shit."

I want to kiss her right now. She believes me? No one ever believes me. Not my father, not my mother, not Kira. Well, to be fair, I never believed Kira either.

"I swear to God I'm going to find him even if it's the last thing I do."

"Honestly, I'm more pissed that he dumped Gidget. Who cares about a sex tape? It's not your first one. And I don't have any family to embarrass. We look amazing in that video, and I'm not ashamed of having sex. I'm a tattoo artist, not a nun. If anything, it will bring publicity to the rescue."

What the fuck? I narrow my gaze at her. Why is she so flippant about this? Most women would freak. Then again, Kira didn't.

My suspicions are triggered, and, for a second, I wonder if I'm wrong about Hugh. Maybe Yessi did leak this tape.

Fuck, I need a moment.

"I'll get it taken care of and get my lawyers to try to get it taken down. Can you head to the store while I deal with this?"

"Sure. Take your time." She walks into the bathroom and shuts the door.

I don't understand her reaction to this situation at all.

Something's off to me. Maybe I've read her wrong. My mind is so twisted that I can't think straight.

I look at my phone and see a text.

Hugh: Meet me at the store.

CHAPTER TWENTY-THREE

YESSI

I arrive at the store and Avril greets me with a hug.

"Damn, girl. You are a freak. I'm so proud. Jealous, but proud. Did you leak the video?"

I roll my eyes. "No, I didn't leak the video. We think Hugh did it."

"Hugh? Really? What an asshole."

Eden encroaches on our conversation. "For real. If he did it, he should go to jail. You're a victim of a sex crime, Yessi."

I laugh. "Yeah, maybe. But I don't care. Like at all. I'm the first person to stand up for any woman who has been sexually assaulted or raped, but, for some reason, this doesn't really bother me."

Avril nods. "It wouldn't bother me, either."

Eden shakes her head. "Well, it would bother me. It's illegal and an invasion of your privacy. Fuck Hugh, seriously. How are you not upset by this? Millions of people have now seen you naked and having sex. You should be outraged."

"I know. I mean, in theory, I should be. But I don't feel that way. I love Preston. In fact, we told both finally said I love you. He said it first. He's everything to me. All I care about is that we're happy, and we are saving animals.

Eden's face tells me that she does not like my answer. "Well, Hugh needs to be arrested. Your flippant attitude is shocking to me."

I don't want to argue with Eden. "Yeah, I get it. More I think about it, it's wrong. I guess just in the scheme of my life, it's not the worst thing that has happened to me." I close my eyes and remember my childhood. I quickly open them again and try to shake off the memories.

Eden hugs me. "I love you, Yessi. You know that. But you should really talk to someone. You may be fine now, but this is not okay."

I hear a knock at the back door. Avril opens it and a drop-dead gorgeous man with wisps of dark hair poking out under a wide-brimmed hat holding a pure-bred black pug smiles at us. He is dressed in a white dress shirt, black pants, and suspenders.

"I'm Jedidah Lapp from Amish Puppies Direct. I have your new shipment of puppies."

What the fuck? I look around for a horse-drawn carriage but instead see a van. The Amish don't drive. Am I being punked?

Avril pushes me out of the way. "Well, hello Jedidah. I like your hat. I'm Avril Peet. But we didn't order any puppies. We are a rescue only store. There must be a mistake."

"There's no mistake, ma'am. I have an order here. Signed yesterday by a Mr. Preston Evans." He points to his clipboard.

I pull the clipboard out of his hands, and there I see it. It's a scanned pdf dated three days ago—with Preston's signature.

Has Preston been lying to me all along? Did he just use me to get the rescue to back the store, so I would call off the rescue protestors, and he would get good press?

Did he leak the tape himself? Did he leak Kira's also?

His father's words ring in my head.

"Is she your girlfriend or just another one of the girls you use and discard?"

Oh my God. I'm such a fool.

Doubt crashes around me. Preston doesn't love me. He's using me. I'm so so stupid. I walked into this trap the day I met him.

I have to get out of here. I can't hear another word.

I run out of the store, climb into my car, and just drive aimlessly.

My phone begins to blow up. Avril. Preston. Eden. But I don't want to listen to anyone. Not Preston's lies. Or Avril's sympathy. Or Eden's judgment.

I just want to be alone. Not only at this moment. But always.

CHAPTER TWENTY-FOUR

PRESTON

I pull up to the store and see a large van parked in the back with the words Amish Puppies Direct on it.

What the fuck? I didn't order any more puppies.

Avril and Eden are animatedly talking to some Amish looking dude, but Yessi is nowhere to be found.

"What's going on here? I'm Preston Evans, the owner of the store. Who are you?"

He shakes my hand. "Nice to meet you. I'm Jedidah Lapp from Amish Puppies Direct. I have them puppies you ordered."

My head hurts from confusion. "I didn't order any

puppies."

"Sir, I have an order from you here."

He shows me a wrinkled order form with an order for twenty puppies of various breeds and my signature at the bottom.

"That's my signature, but I didn't sign it."

"I spoke with you two weeks ago. We picked out the puppies, and then you finalized the form this week."

"Two weeks ago, I was in Hawai'i. I've never spoken to you." But clearly, he spoke to someone else.

And that person could only be Hugh.

Speak of the devil, Hugh walks into the store with a huge smirk on his face.

He pats me on the back. "You can thank me later, Evans. I just saved your store from this rescue bullshit."

Oh hell no. I run up to him and slam him against the wall.

"What the fuck did you do, you motherfucker? Did you leak that sex tape of Yessi and me? Of Kira and me? Did you dump Gidget in the night drop? Did you order these fucking puppies? I'm going to fucking kill you. Answer me, dammit."

"Yeah, I fucking did. I made you, asshole. Before the sex tape with Kira, you were nothing. You keep falling in love with these hot chicks, and once you get high on their pussies, you can't think straight. Have you seen Doggy Style's Yelp reviews? We have been slammed by so many customers. People want purebreds, not mangy mutts like that stupid dog Gidget. She peed on my leg, so I dumped her. Now tell these two bitches to leave the store, and we can get back to business."

I clench my fist and sock him in the jaw. "I'm calling the cops on you. I've been making excuses for your ass for years. I'm done. You are dead to me."

"Whatever, dude. You will get over it. And you are not going to press charges. I own half this business, remember? I doubt these rescue chicks can bail you out."

Fuck. He's right about that. But I'd rather have no business than work with this guy. "You're dead to me."

"Whatever, Evans. You'll come crawling back. I'll check in with you later, once Yessi leaves your sorry ass. I'll be in touch." He walks out of the store. I'm tempted to run after him and give him a proper beat down but decide it will best to let the authorities handle it.

I need to find Yessi.

"Where's Yessi?"

"She left," Avril says. "You're a good man, Evans. I believe you about the puppies. But what are we going to do now? We can't send them back? They will be resold."

"I agree. We can fix them like we did the others and then adopt them out. At least they won't be bred."

Eden is playing with the black pug puppy. "Yeah. We have to keep them—especially this one. But from now on, no more puppies."

"Well, I don't think there will be a from now on. Hugh's right. He's a co-owner. I have to find someone to buy him out."

"So you want the puppies or not?" Jedidah asks.

"We'll keep them. Hey, why are you driving a van? I thought it was against your religion."

"It is. But I'm on Rumspringa. I haven't been baptized by the church yet. I'm just helping my pop out."

Avril's eyes grow wide. "Rumspringa? So you can fuck?"

Jedidah smiles. "Most definitely. Let's go now."

Eden just shakes her head. "Jesus, Avril. He's a fucking puppy breeder."

"Yeah, but he's hot. Hey, I mean Yessi fucked Preston. He was opening a puppy store. If she converted him, I could convert Jedidah."

I laugh. "Man, you are all nuts. Jedidah, how much do I owe you?"

He tells me, and I pay him.

"Ladies, can you handle the store and the puppies. I need to find Yessi."

Avril is fawning over Jedidah. "Of course. Maybe Jedidah can hang around for a few nights and help me out."

He tips his hat. "I'd like that."

Eden throws up her hands. "Am I in the twilight zone? Am I the only sane person left here?"

"Yup," I say. "I'm going to go find Yessi."

I get in my truck and call Yessi. It goes straight to voice-mail. I keep calling and calling, but she won't answer. Where is she?

I check her Instagram praying for a sign. Nothing.

I think. Where could she be? And then it comes to me.

I race down the freeway and exit at the animal shelter.

CHAPTER TWENTY-FIVE

YESSI

I walk around the shelter, looking at all the helpless dogs that are about to die. Here I thought I was making a difference and saving dogs. But instead, I helped a man sell puppies.

I'm weak. I fell for Preston Evans. He used me to promote his puppy store. I was so desperate for love that I believed what he said.

And now, I have nothing to show for it. I quit my job at the tattoo parlor, I moved out of my place. Hell, even my dogs are with Avril. I'm so pathetic.

I reach my hand in a kennel and pet an old dog. He looks like a lab/corgi with a long short body and turned out toes. He has no shot of surviving.

I break into sobs.

I hear footsteps behind me. I'm afraid to turn around. Is it the kennel tech with a red leash about to lead him to his death?

"Yessi."

Preston? I slowly turn around and just leap into his arms, despite myself.

"Yessi, babe. I'm here."

I pull eye and stare at him. "Did you leak the tape? Did you order those puppies? Don't you lie to me."

"No. I didn't. I swear to you. I would never lie to you."

I want to believe him so badly. "Then who did?"

"Hugh. He showed up at the store just now. He admitted to everything. I'm going to press charges about the tapes."

As pathetic as it sounds, I believe Preston. Since we have been together, he has been totally open and honest with me. Sure, I doubted him, but I can't believe he would order puppies after all we have been through.

"What about the puppies? Did you send them back? Dude will probably drown them."

"Well, Avril, Eden, and I agreed we should just fix them and adopt them out, so they aren't bred. Last puppies ever though, I promise. You can be in charge of picking dogs. I have to find a way to keep the store open. I need to come up with the cash to buy out Hugh."

Ugh. "How much cash?"

"The loan was for four hundred thousand dollars."

Jesus. I will never see that money in my lifetime.

"So, it's hopeless?"

He smirks. "Nah. I'm sure the two of us can find a way to get sponsors if the store is only for rescue dogs. Don't give up on me, Yessi. I need you."

It feels so good to be needed. "I need you, too."

"Meanwhile, Avril has the hots for the Amish guy. She thinks she can convert him like you converted me."

"**P**res, your parents are here."

I kiss Yessi. "Thanks, babe."

I walk out of my office and see my father talking to Yessi, and my mother is browsing in the store.

"Hey, Dad."

"Hey, Son."

We embrace and briefly catch up. It's hard to believe that a year ago we weren't even on speaking terms. So much has changed since then.

After Hugh was arrested, my father finally forgave me. But it took me a while to come around because I still had resentment toward him because he didn't believe me. But

Yessi kept pushing us to work out our differences. After a few therapy sessions, my father and I hashed it out. And now he's the co-owner of the Pugs N Roses rescue boutique. We changed the name from Doggy Style after cutting all ties with Hugh, who is currently in jail.

Dad still lives in Hawai'i but is spending time here. And he adopted Cuffs. Those two are thick as thieves.

I also apologized to Kira for blaming her about leaking the tape, and thankfully she forgave me. Not that she can be bothered with commoners like me—she's dating a prince.

Avril took off with Jedidah back to Amish country. I don't even know what's up with her because she doesn't call. Can't really blame her—the Amish don't even have phones.

Eden is still happily single and helping out in the store when she can.

As for Yessi and I, we are so happy together. She is truly my soulmate. I adopted Gidget and sold my condo. Yessi and I moved to a farmhouse where we could have all her pets. We live on two acres of land and even had to get a kennel license. But I love our home.

And the store has been thriving. We have adopted out over one thousand shelter pets in one year.

I grab Yessi's hand and take her over by the front door, where we first met.

"Excuse me, ladies and gentlemen. A year ago today, this gorgeous woman handcuffed herself to this door to get me to stop selling puppies. Honestly, I thought she was crazy. And hot, but mostly crazy. But now I think she wasn't the crazy one, I was. She has opened my eyes up to so many things, made me a better man, repaired my relationship with my family, and changed my life. Now I want to make her my wife."

I pull the ring out of my pocket and drop to my knees.

Yessi gasps.

"Will you marry me?"

"Oh my God, Pres. Yes!"

I place the ring on her finger and kiss her as the store erupts in applause.

I whisper in her ear. "I have one more surprise."

I grab the handcuffs that she used a year ago on the door and handcuff her to me.

She laughs. "I've been wondering where those were."

I kiss my fiancée. "I told you I'd save them for later."

Though this book is a work of fiction, it is based on my time running my dog rescue, **Pugs N Roses**.

We have saved close to 400 dogs from high kill shelters in Southern California.

Please adopt a dog from a rescue or a shelter. Never breed or buy. We have amazing dogs, including purebreeds and puppies.

Also, please consider giving a donation to Pugs N Roses. We are a 501 3 c non profit and 100% of the donations go to the veterinary care of the animals in our care.

Thank you for reading my book.
If you liked it, would you please consider leaving a
review? **Doggy Style**

*Please stay tuned for the next two books in the Rescue Me
series,* **Downward Dog** *and* **Tail Chaser***.*

For the latest updates, release, and giveaways, subscribe to
Alana's newsletter. Sign up today to receive two
free books.

For all her available books, check out Alana's **website** or
Facebook page.

Follow me on **Bookbub**.

Stay Tuned for an excerpt of my book ***Blue Sky***.

DOWNWARD DOG

RESCUE ME #2

Kira

You've followed my Instagram, you've watched my sex tape, you think you know all about me.

I'm Kira Morgan. Celebrity yoga instructor turned tabloid kicking toy. I lost everything when the sex tape with my ex-boyfriend, Preston, was leaked to the press by his shady best friend. Producers on my reality show fired me, my boyfriend left me, and my reputation had gone to the dogs. Only my rescue beagle Lady has remained loyal to me.

When I meet Britain's bad boy Prince Henry, I refuse to give him the time of the day. It doesn't matter that he's gorgeous, charming, compassionate, and rich. I won't get involved in a high-profile relationship. All I want is my privacy.

But when he asks me to teach yoga at his charity fundraiser, I agree. All the money will go to save dogs, like my Lady, from laboratories.

One week and I never have to see this handsome, dirty-talking prince again.

I don't want his diamond ring but I'm happy to play with his royal jewels.

I may want him but I can never be part of his life. I won't allow myself to be labeled a Royal Bitch.

Preorder Downward Dog Now

Available February 5, 2019

Avril

Jedidah Lapp is the most eligible man in Lancaster County. He's six foot two, gorgeous, and famous for his stint on the Amish reality show, Bad Amish. I hate him. I hate his stupid puppy mill, Amish Puppies Direct. I hate the way he looks at me like I'm his breeding bitch. I don't care that his abs are chiseled, his arms are ripped, and his face belongs on the cover of a magazine. Every dog bred means a shelter dog dead!

After going to a puppy auction, I decide to go undercover Amish to stop his breeding facility. But once he finds out my identity, he throws me a bone.

If I spend one week with him before he decides if he

should be baptized Amish, he will stop breeding dogs, saving thousands of dogs' lives.

One week and I never have to see this sexy, dirty-talking jerk again. He can't stop chasing my tail, but he makes me act like a bitch in heat.

Preorder Tail Chaser Now

Available May 14, 2019

BLUE SKY EXCERPT

THERE'S A BRIGHT LINING TO EVERY DARK CLOUD.

For ten weeks every year, the Blue Angels descend from the heavens and land in heEl Centro, California. The residents treat the pilots like gods. The city council members host black tie galas, little old ladies bring them homemade pies, and groupies wait by their rooms to satisfy their desires. Everyone worships them—everyone, that is, except for me. I hate the way they waltz into my poor town and romance all the residents only to vanish into the sky.

But even I can't afford to say no when I'm offered the chance to be the nanny for sexy, cocky pilot Beckett Daly's baby girl, Sky. The job is my only hope to feed my family and maybe one day leave this town.

No matter how close I grow to Beckett, no matter how much I hunger for his embrace, I'll never let down my guard for this Devil in a Blue Angel's disguise.

I stood in my mama's kitchen, peeling back the husks of the ripe tomatillos my neighbor had gifted to me. Even though I lived only miles away from the Mexican border, fresh produce was expensive and purchasing my beloved tart, green fruit was definitely a luxury I couldn't afford.

Not when there was a constant, gnawing ache in my belly. Not when my little sister Ana María cried every morning because she wanted more food, but I had none to give her. Not when my other sister, Mónica, would often eat her only meal of the day at school because she had free lunch. Not when I had to feed a family of four on fifty dollars a week.

If only I had a job.

But my employment status wasn't from a lack of effort. No, not at all. I had literally applied to every job in the border town of El Centro, California, which had just recently been anointed "the worst place to live in America" by some huge national website. With the highest unemployment rate in the country at twenty-seven and a half percent, my prospects were bleak. I lay awake most nights, terror gripping my body, shivering despite the sweltering desert heat, trapped in the hell that was my life, dreaming of an escape route.

In reality, I doubted that I would ever be able to leave my hometown. Instead, I would probably end up being buried here, but these days, even *that* wasn't a certainty. El Centro's cemetery had recently gone into foreclosure.

I clutched the tomatillos in my hands, rinsed them under the cool water, cut out their stems, and tossed them in a pan to roast. This spicy sauce would coat the chicken enchiladas I had just made from scratch. Accompanied by a pot of cumin-spiced pinto beans and a batch of *arroz rojo*, we would be blessed with a rare, hearty dinner. Over the years, I had learned how to make delicious meals out of scraps. These enchiladas, along with oatmeal for breakfast and tortillas for lunch, would have to last my family for a week.

Ana María walked into the kitchen and clutched on my apron. "Where's Mama?"

At six years old, Ana María was a precocious little girl with amber-colored eyes and long brown hair that I made sure to braid every day, since Mama was usually too hungover to move, and that was if she even came home from her one of her frequent benders. Ana María was too young to learn the truth about our lives, though I knew I wouldn't be able to protect her forever.

"Baby, she's out working." And that was true, in a way. But Mama didn't have a real job, either. Her version of "working" was flirting with men at the local bars and offering them favors for a bit of cash.

"I am not a prostitute," Mama would swear up and down. "I just love men."

I didn't even try to argue with her anymore. The fact that Mama had three children with three different men, none of whom she'd married, let her decisions speak for herself. Not that there was anything wrong with a woman enjoying a healthy sex life. But she lavished attention on these countless men while she neglected her children, which was deplorable.

At least I didn't know who my father was, so I could sometimes close my eyes and pretend that he was a good man. Maybe he didn't even know I existed and if he found out that he had a daughter, he would rush to me and take me away from my mom.

If only Mama would tell me his name, I would be able to find him.

But my fantasy dad was the only good man in my life. Mónica's father was a dead beat and a womanizer who had cheated on Mama all the time before she'd kicked his sorry ass out. And Ana María's father was a hot-tempered alcoholic who would beat Mama until she could cry no more. The only other man around was my uncle, who also waged a losing battle with the bottle.

But growing up around these jerks, none of whom stuck around, told me all I needed to know about men.

Men were trouble. Untrustworthy. Only after one thing. At twenty years old, I was proud to say that I had never been distracted by a man, even though my soft curves and plump lips often made me a target for their leers. Sure, I had messed around with boys in high school and had even lost my virginity to a good friend of mine who had wanted to date me, but I told him that I was not looking for a relationship. I vowed that I would never let any man get in the way of my dreams of leaving this town, and this life, behind.

But Mama had never known another way of living. She'd been only eighteen when she had become pregnant with me. Did Mama once have dreams of her own? Mama used to tell me, *"El sueño es alimento de los pobres."*

Dreams are the food of the poor.

Mama's future had blown away with the dust in this desert town. But my dreams were still real. Sometimes I closed my eyes and practiced creative visualization, something I had read about in a book. I pictured myself running a successful restaurant, living in a cute apartment, even owning a car. But no matter how hard I tried, I couldn't fathom a scenario where I would get an opportunity to change my life.

I just need a break.

I sat Ana María down in front of a coloring book and turned my attention back to the salsa. I sliced half a white onion while blinking back the tears that were not only from the vapors but also from my despair. After I pulled myself together, I crushed two garlic cloves, chopped fifteen sprigs of cilantro, and halved and de-stemmed a serrano pepper.

My tomatillos were now ready, and when I removed them from the oven, their smoky scent filled up the tiny kitchen. I chopped the tomatillos and grabbed the *molcajete* to grind the salsa when my other sister, Mónica, burst into the room.

"Paloma, Paloma!" Mónica shrieked.

"What?" At fourteen, Mónica was definitely the rebel of the family, and already boy-crazy. I worried that Mónica would end up just like our mother. To make certain that she didn't, I'd forced her to go on birth control this year. If only I could take custody of my sisters and get out of this town.

"OMG! Look at this!" She thrust a copy of the *Imperial Press* in my face.

"Ay, Mónica." I did not have time to read some gut-wrenching story in the newspaper. Just last week one of my high school classmates had been murdered in her apartment, which was only one street over from ours. The cops suspected drug traffickers, but it didn't matter. Another reminder that the only way out of this town was in a body bag.

"It's your dream job!"

Dream job? My dream was any job—I'd clean toilets, I'd

mop floors, no job was below me. But with no car and nothing but a high school education, my prospects were bleak. And we needed the money now even more desperately than ever. The little help my mom received from the government went to food, and the rest was often squandered by her on alcohol. I choked back a sob. I didn't know how much longer we could all survive like this.

I grabbed the paper cautiously, refusing to get my hopes up again.

Looking for a full time live in nanny for my daughter. I'll be stationed in El Centro for ten weeks. Must be CPR certified. No drugs and no drama. Pay is $1000 a week. Will be taking applications in person January 4th at 4 p.m. at the Navy Lodge, El Centro, room 101.

I dropped the *temolote* I had been using to grind the salsa from my right hand. Did that say one *thousand* dollars a week for ten weeks?

Ten thousand dollars?

That money could be life-changing for my sisters and me. I could move the girls to San Diego and leave my mother and her destructive ways behind. I could rent a small apartment and send them to school out there, even get a job at a local restaurant to support them.

I stared at the old clock that hung on our cracked wall. It was quarter past two. The Navy Lodge was a few miles away, so I would have to leave enough time to walk. *Ay, Dios mío*, what would I wear?

I turned to Mónica and grabbed her shoulders. "*¡Ayudeme!* I need you to watch Ana María and pick me out an outfit. Something simple and classy. Nothing tight. I'm going to finish these enchiladas and bring them to the interview. Do *not* tell Mama where I went if she decides to come home."

Mónica's face dropped as she gazed longingly at the enchiladas. "Our enchiladas? What will we eat?"

"Beans and rice and tortillas. Military men like to eat. These enchiladas could be our ticket."

"*Sí, entiendo.* You got this. You're great with kids. If he hires you, I'll help out completely back here, no attitude, I swear."

My hand shook. How would this even work if I got this job? Who would take care of my sisters? My mom wasn't reliable. My only option was my uncle, but he was a goddamn mess. For ten thousand dollars and a way out of this town, we could make it work.

Mónica tilted her head. "I wonder if he's an Angel? I bet he's smoking hot."

A Blue Angel pilot . . . he had to be if he was offering one thousand dollars a week. No enlisted man in the support team of the Angels would pay that much money. A little girl? Where was her mother? Was she dead? Or just a dead beat like my mom?

For ten weeks every year, the Blue Angels descended from the heavens and landed in El Centro. The Angels were notorious as much for their sky stunts as they were for their land antics. They would hit the bars here, romancing the young local Mexican girls who dreamed of a life as a naval aviator's wife. It was like the *sucia* version of *An Officer and a Gentleman,* minus the happy ending; no Blue Angel had ever married a local girl.

But I didn't want to fall in love. I didn't believe in love. I had never experienced anything even close to love. I wanted a job. I needed a job. A job that could put food on the table, give me enough money to flee this town, and save my sisters from this fate.

My hand shook as I picked back up my *temolote* and finished grinding the ingredients. I dipped my finger into the *molcajete* and sampled my *salsa verde.* The delicious green sauce was perfectly spicy, yet tangy. I spread the mixture over the chicken enchiladas, crafted with home-made tortillas and lots of love, just like my late *abuela* had taught me. All of the lovers that Mama brought home couldn't get enough of my cooking. *Abuelita* would always say, *"Un hombre se conquista por el estómago."* The way to a man's heart was through his stomach. Maybe that was why Mama could never keep a man—she couldn't cook at all.

There would be hundreds of women, and possibly even men, applying for this job. I was amazing with kids and had pretty much raised my sisters myself. Even so, I needed an edge.

When they were in town, these Angels would haunt the local restaurants, devouring the native cuisine. *Carne asada burritos, carnitas adobadas, chile verde, tacos el carbon*—those rich white boys couldn't get enough of our food. Maybe my cooking could truly be my ticket to a new life.

I grabbed a copy of my résumé from the bookshelf and placed it in my purse. Mónica walked back into the kitchen, holding Mama's best dress, a navy-blue sheath with white trim. It was usually reserved for church, which was why it was in good shape. Mama hated to attend for fear she would be judged. A fear in this small town with my mom's shameless behavior that was definitely warranted.

I slipped it over my head and looked at myself in the bathroom mirror; the reflection of a tired, slim, and desperate girl staring right back at me. Well, at least the dress fit perfectly—not too tight or too baggy.

Mónica grabbed a little bag under the sink. "Let me do your makeup."

I shook my head. "No, this is a job interview, not a date."

"Right. And you need to look your best. Give me five minutes."

I gave up and let her have her way with me. I needed this job so badly it hurt. As Mónica started applying foundation, I exhaled and did something I hadn't done in years.

I prayed.

Once a devout Catholic, I had stopped going to church when my *abuela* died after being hit by a drunk driver. My *abuela* hadn't even been that old at only fifty-five. Without her guidance, we Pérez girls had fallen apart. Mama only cared about herself, and now it was up to me to be the adult in the household.

After a few more agonizing minutes of Mónica dabbing, blotting, and painting my skin, she finally released me.

"Look at yourself! You're beautiful. I would definitely hire you to watch my baby."

I looked in the mirror again, and this time I saw how green my eyes looked enhanced by the purple shadow and how my curled eyelashes made me appear awake even when I was getting by on only hours of sleep.

But more importantly, I saw an expression I hadn't seen in the mirror since I'd given up my college scholarship because I was afraid of how my sisters would survive without me.

I saw hope.

CHAPTER 2

I t wasn't supposed to be like this.

My beautiful wife, Catherine, should be sitting here with me now, playing with our little girl, deeply entrenched in the joys of motherhood.

We had been so excited to spend these ten weeks in El Centro with our daughter, Sky. Ten weeks that we would've been able to spend together without me having to fly to other cities for airshows. Catherine and I couldn't wait to return to this tragic town that, despite having so little resources, had welcomed us with open arms. I couldn't wait to come home every night to my wife and child. I had dreamed of bonding with our daughter before I had to leave her again every week to entertain the public by doing aerial tricks.

Now, spending time with my little girl was the only dream I had left.

I pulled back the curtains in my room at the Navy Lodge and jerked my head back when I saw that the line was wrapped around the entire hotel. There were men, women, even teenagers outside, all desperate for a chance to make a living in this border town.

I should forget this stupid idea.

Sure, I could've hired a nanny to travel with me from one of those fancy agencies. And I had definitely considered it. The ones I had interviewed had impressive résumés, but they had lacked heart. None of them seemed to truly need or even want to watch my baby.

I also could've left Sky back at home with Catherine's parents, who had pretty much taken care of her alone last year while I'd flown around the country for four days a week. But I had made a promise to my wife when she had been dying. A promise that I wouldn't leave Sky somewhere else to be raised when I was stationed somewhere for a few months. A promise that I would give someone the opportunity of a lifetime.

An even more importantly, I didn't want to be away from Sky any longer than I had to.

It had been my wife's idea to place an ad in El Centro's newspaper. We had lived here together last year, and Sky had been born in this town. Catherine had loved the warmth of the people here, their hard work ethic, their perseverance in the face of adversity. When she'd had only moments to live, she'd made me promise that I would find a nanny out here when I returned. And dammit, I was a man of my word. Especially to her.

But how was I going to choose?

Sky cooed in the corner, happy in her swing. She was a happy, chubby baby, and thankfully a good sleeper, though recently she had been restless at night because she was teething. Since moving back here a week ago, the officers' wives had taken shifts helping to care for her when I was at work. I was grateful for their support, but it did nothing to soothe the ache in my heart from losing the love of my life. But as much as I was certain that I would never love again, I missed being around women. Their scent, their touch, their taste. My friends' wives had offered to set me up with their single friends, but I had no interest in dating. And the idea of having a one-night stand held no appeal to me. I needed to set a good example for my little girl and hooking up with random women I had no intention of getting serious with was not a step in the right direction.

Even so, I felt guilty that she didn't have a mommy. A woman in her life that would love her the way Catherine did. Her grandparents and I adored her, but we were no substitute for a mother's love.

I picked Sky up, planted a kiss on her forehead and took her into the other room where I rocked her to sleep and then placed her in her crib. Once she was out, I quietly exited the room.

As an officer, I was used to taking control and had already planned a strategy for today. Most importantly, I wanted someone who clearly loved children and didn't just see this as a job.

I was going to ask everyone the same question. *What are you going to do with the money?* And I knew exactly what I was looking for in that answer. I wanted someone who was selfless, wanted to help others, and had a clear plan of exactly what they would do with the money. I wanted to change someone's life.

My buddy, Sawyer, opened the door to my room. "Ready?"

"Yup. Let them in."

Sawyer had offered to be crowd control. He was also an Angel, but—unlike me—Sawyer was a womanizer. He had a girl in every city. Not that I could blame him—Blue Angels really were the rock stars of the air. But that kind of life had never appealed to me. Catherine had been my high school sweetheart. We had dated long-distance when I attended the U.S. Naval Academy in Annapolis, and after I had graduated, we were married in the chapel. She had been a great wife. She had been faithful to me during my many deployments to the Middle East, had never once complained as I chased my dreams, supported me fully even when we had spent years apart. All of our future plans had been cruelly ripped from us in what was supposed to be the happiest time of our life. All I had left of Catherine was our baby. And I would do everything in my power to give her the life Catherine wanted for her.

The first batch of people shuffled through the room one at a time, repeating their similar tragic life stories. Out of work for years, the money would go to feed their children, get out of debt, pay for medical bills. But with none of them did I truly think that this opportunity would change their lives. It seemed instead like a Band-Aid. And once the money ran out, they would be stuck in the same place they were before they had this job. I thanked every one of them and told them I would contact them tomorrow if they were chosen. Even my numb heart ached at the despair in these confessions. Maybe I had been wrong.

Maybe I wouldn't be able to choose. Maybe I wouldn't find what I was needed.

I closed my eyes and prayed to the heavens. "Please, Catherine. Help me out here. Give me a sign. Something."

After about an hour more of interviews, I had begun to lose hope. Then a girl with an incredible body entered the room. Her jet-black hair framed her angelic face, and her pale green eyes gazed at me over the casserole dish she was holding. I forced myself not to undress her with my eyes, but I couldn't help but notice how incredibly beautiful she was. She handed me a résumé and then cautiously peeled back the tin foil, and the scent of roasted tomatillos, corn tortillas, and cheese filled the air.

My eyes widened when I saw the enchiladas verdes. My favorite. Catherine and I had spent last winter trying every Mexican restaurant in El Centro on a quest for the best enchiladas. Was this my sign?

"Hello, sir. My name is Paloma Pérez. I would be honored to apply for the nanny position. I'm a hard worker, and I love babies. I've raised my sisters pretty much myself. I was also valedictorian of my high school class, and I am CPR certified. And I cook, too. I'd be happy to cook for you every day. Would you like to try these enchiladas? I made them from scratch—even the tortillas and the sauce, which is made with fresh, roasted tomatillos."

My stomach rumbled, and my mouth watered in anticipation of this home-cooked meal. I had been existing on fast food, ramen, and pizza since my wife had passed, but I needed to get my act in gear for the upcoming season. I had to be one hundred-percent focused on flying, or my fellow pilots could be killed. Even worse, I could crash into a crowd of innocent spectators. After Catherine had died, the Navy had offered to give my slot to another pilot, but I had quickly shot down that idea. No way. I had worked toward this dream my entire life. Catherine would be livid if I stopped living my life to mourn her. I had to push forward, no matter how much it hurt. For Catherine. For Sky.

"I'd love to. Thank you, Paloma. I'm Beckett Daly. Nice to meet you."

Paloma's face brightened into a smile, and she looked around the room's kitchenette. "Can I get you a plate? A drink? I would've brought something. I'm so sorry."

"Hey, don't apologize. I'll get the plates." I stood up and grabbed two plates from the cupboard, utensils, and a wide spatula. I fought the urge to pop open a beer in front of her and instead reached for two glasses, which I filled with water. After I served the food, I sat down at the table and invited Paloma to sit next to me.

I dug my fork into the enchiladas, and the second the bite hit my mouth, my taste buds were in heaven. The enchiladas were not too mild, not too hot. Just perfectly spiced, tart, and fresh. Before I could come up for air, I took another bite, and then another. I devoured one of the enchiladas on my plate and became completely lost in this amazing dish. For the first time since my wife had died, I felt satisfied. Catherine would've loved them.

But she couldn't. She was dead. And here I was gorging myself on this applicant's food, enjoying this delectable dish, feeling happy.

Hell, I felt guilty eating enchiladas without Catherine.

I pushed back my plate.

"These are delicious."

"Thank you, Mr. Daly."

"I go by Beck. Where did you learn to cook?"

"My grandmother taught me. I love to cook. I can make anything you like to eat. All the Mexican specialties, of course—flautas, burritos, tacos. But I can learn anything else you like—hamburgers, spaghetti, meatloaf. You name it, I'll make it."

Her desperation hung thick in the air, and I wasn't ignorant to the fact that there were still at least a hundred other people in line. I had to give everyone a chance, but I was entranced by the girl sitting in front of me. And I'd be lying if I didn't admit that I was insanely attracted to her, despite myself.

"So, tell me, Paloma, how would you spend your day with my daughter, Sky? She's nine months old."

She grinned. "Oh. I love that age. We would have so much fun. I don't believe in any screen time, and I don't watch television. We would sing songs, play games, take walks around the base, go to the park. I would read to her every day and go to the library. I'd be available for any playdates with any other babies on base. And I have this Mommy and Me yoga video I used to do with my sister. Ana María loved it."

I winced. Catherine had bought a bunch of Mommy and Me yoga DVDs. She had dreamed of doing them with Sky. It had completely slipped my mind until Paloma mentioned it.

Yoga. Another sign.

But I wasn't convinced yet.

"What would you do with the money you would earn as my daughter's nanny?"

She gulped and took a deep breath. "I'll be honest with you, sir. My mom is a mess. She had me when she was very young, she drinks and runs around with men. I take care of my two sisters, and we often don't have enough food to eat. They are good girls, but I worry about their future. I want them to go to college. There aren't any jobs around here in El Centro. I have a high school degree, but I turned down my college scholarship because I just couldn't abandon my sisters here with my mom."

Her voice cracked, and I was worried that she would cry. Paloma had just said that her family was hungry, yet she had given me food.

She spoke rapidly, as if she had interpreted my silence as a reason to up the ante. "I would take the money and move to San Diego. Leave this town forever. It would be enough to get a tiny studio apartment. We are used to being crammed into one room. I would get a job and attend college part-time. It would be a struggle, but we would make it work." She paused and bit her lip. "Please give me a chance, sir. I won't disappoint you. This opportunity would change my life."

Bam. And there it was. The sign I had been waiting for hit me over the head like the sound of thunder crashing on my plane. I had struggled with my faith daily since my wife had died, and Paloma's presence had just forced me to remind myself that even though I was in deep pain, I was blessed. I had a great career, a beautiful daughter, had been married to a wonderful, loving wife, and had food to eat. Had Catherine sent our baby girl and me this message?

"I hope this isn't inappropriate, but do you have a boyfriend? I'm not interested in having any drama."

"No, sir. I don't have a boyfriend, or any desire to have one. I don't date at all. My only focus is on taking care of my sisters and getting a job."

I paused. Her sisters. If her mom was so irresponsible, who would watch them if she took this job?

"This is a live-in nanny position. You would have to spend the night. Who would watch your sisters?"

"Oh, you don't have to worry about my sisters. They would stay with my uncle. I've spoken to my sister, Mónica, who is fourteen, and she has agreed to step up and help with our youngest sister, Ana María, who is six, if I am blessed enough to get this job."

She bit her lip when she mentioned her uncle, and I wondered if she was lying about him being able to take care of them. She had also mentioned turning down a college scholarship to take care of her sisters. Couldn't her uncle have watched them then? Maybe he was willing to take care of them for ten weeks, but not for four years.

My heart constricted in my chest. I had gotten her hopes up. I couldn't let her down now. But I had to let her know what she was in for by working for me. And I had to see if she would be good with Sky.

"You would have to be up at night to take care of Sky. I would love to get up with her, but I have to have a good night's sleep, or I can't fly. Your room would be on the opposite side of the home. Would you be okay with that?"

She nodded her head vigorously and then lifted her eyes which met mine. As they locked in intensity, I felt, even if only for a moment, like we shared a deep connection. "Yes, sir, that would be wonderful. You won't hear a peep out of me. And I will do my best to keep her quiet."

"When I come home from work, I would like some time alone with my daughter. You will be free to go home for a few hours and see your sisters, which could work out because it would be after school. I keep to myself most days, and to be honest with you, I'm not a pleasure to be around. My wife passed away nine months ago."

A lump grew in my throat, and I stopped talking. Nine months. Had it been almost a year? Why did every second without Catherine seem like an eternity? If living without her for nine months had been so painful, how could I bear to spend the rest of my life without her?

I wasn't ready to express my grief to this girl. "I don't mean to be rude, but I have no interest in being your friend. Our relationship must be strictly business."

"Yes, sir. I understand completely. I won't bother you at all. If I'm given this job, I will just be so grateful for the opportunity."

Sawyer opened the door. "Beck, the line is getting anxious."

"Give me a minute." I turned back to Paloma. "Would you like to meet my daughter?"

"I'd love to."

I opened the door to the bedroom where, despite the noise, little Sky was still sleeping contently. I carefully watched Paloma. Her face lit up when she saw Sky. I didn't sense anything fake about Paloma's smile.

"She's so precious," Paloma whispered, and she knelt down by the crib.

I stood back for a moment to watch Paloma. She kept her gaze on my daughter and didn't even seem to notice that I was still in the room.

I had no more doubts. Deep in my soul, I knew that Paloma was the woman who was meant to be Sky's nanny.

I motioned her to leave the room and grabbed my phone to text Sawyer.

Send them home.

"Paloma, thanks for meeting with me. I'd like to offer you the position, contingent on checking your references."

Paloma stood in front of me, her chin quivering as tears welled in her eyes. "You mean it, sir? Of all these applicants, you choose me? I've never had any luck in my life."

"Yes. I choose you. And it isn't about luck. We are both in the position to help each other. I will still call your references, and I will run a background check, but if everything checks out, you will start in two days. Will everything check out? No convictions? Nothing I should know about? Tell me now, so you don't waste my time."

"No, sir, none. I have lived my life honorably and honestly. I have never done any drugs, never been drunk. I'm determined to make something of myself. I can't thank you enough for giving me this opportunity."

"You're welcome. I have your number, and I'll call you tomorrow afternoon. Thank you for the enchiladas. They were delicious."

Before I could stop her, Paloma flung her arms around my neck. My breath hitched; I hadn't been this close to a woman since my wife died, and I didn't have any desire to cross this line with Sky's nanny. Even so, heat rose in my body, and I imagined slamming her against the wall and fucking her.

Instead, I hugged her back, enjoying the warmth of her tight little body before she pulled back fast.

She averted her eyes, and her cheeks turned a shade of blush. "I'm so sorry, sir. I know that was inappropriate, but I'm just so happy. It won't happen again. This is the best day of my life. Thank you. I won't disappoint you."

My mouth became moist, and I fought the urge to kiss her. Then I read myself the riot act.

Don't fuck the nanny.

I had to break the awkward silence. "Wait. Take the rest of the enchiladas. They were delicious."

"Thank you, sir."

And with that, the beautiful Paloma Pérez walked out of my hotel room, leaving me with my lone enchilada.

Tonight, I'd had my first home-cooked meal since Catherine died. I cracked open a Corona, cut a lime wedge, and pushed it inside the bottle. One sip and my nerves relaxed. Another bite of the gooey enchilada and warmth filled my soul.

I knew Catherine was looking down on me.

Purchase Blue Sky now!

ACKNOWLEDGMENTS

I WOULD LIKE TO THANK my husband, Roger, for all your incredible support and love.

To my boys, Connor and Caleb. I love you both so much. You are the reason for my every smile.

To Nicole Blanchard. For motivating me to write everyday when I didn't want to.

To Joanne Machin for saving me by editing as I go. You are priceless.

To Sara Eirew: For taking this wonderful picture.

To Aria Tan: for the cover.

To Shannon Criss from EverAfter for your endless patience on this book.

ALANA ALBERTSON IS the former President of RWA's Contemporary Romance, Young Adult, and Chick Lit chapters. She holds a M.Ed. from Harvard and a BA in English from Stanford. She lives in San Diego, California, with her husband, two sons, and six rescue dogs. When she's not saving dogs from high kill shelters through her rescue Pugs N Roses, she can be found watching episodes of Cobra Kai, Younger, or Dallas Cowboys Cheerleaders: Making the Team.

Please join my newsletter to receive 2 free books!

Newsletter

Website

Email Me

Facebook Group

Want more romantic reads?

Try my other books!

Rescue Me

Romantic Comedy Series

Doggy Style

Meet Preston! When it comes to doggy style, he's behind you 100%.

Downward Dog

Meet Prince Henry! Prince Henry wants me to assume the position of his royal bitch.

Tail Chaser

Meet Jedidah! He can't stop chasing my tail.

Blue Devils

Military Pilots Contemporary Series

Blue Sky

Meet Beckett! I'll never let down my guard for this Devil in a Blue Angel's disguise.

Snow and Her SEALs

Contemporary Reverse Harem

The Temptation of Snow

Meet Snow's SEALs! *Seven sexy Nave SEALs. Why should I limit myself to just one?*

(co-written with **Lisa London**)

Se7en Deadly SEALs

Navy SEAL Romantic Thriller

Season One:

Conceit, Chronic, Crazed, Carnal, Crave, Consume, Covet

Season One Box Set

Meet Grant! She wants to get wild? I will fulfill her every fantasy.

Season Two:

Smug

Meet Mitch! I'll always be your bad boy.

The Trident Code

Navy SEAL Romantic Suspense Series

Invincible

Meet Pat! I had one chance to put on the cape and be her hero.

Invaluable

Meet Kyle! I'll never win MVP, never get a championship ring, but some heroes don't play games.

Heroes Ever After

Military New Adult Fairy Tale Retellings

Beast

Meet Grady! With tattooed arms sculpted from carrying M-16s, this bad boy has girls begging from sea to shining sea to get a piece of his action.

Triton

Meet Erik! I'm a Navy SEAL, a Triton, a god of the sea.

And she will never be part of my world.

Dance with Me

Swing

Meet Bret! He was a real man—muscles sculpted from carrying weapons, not from practicing pilates.

Sway

Meet Tony! The long haired rock and roll drummer with a boyish grin.

Military Contemporary Stand Alone

Badass

Meet Shane! I'm America's cockiest badass.

(co-written with **Linda Barlow**)

CPSIA information can be obtained
at www.ICGtesting.com
Printed in the USA
BVHW07s1122091018
529682BV00001B/102/P